Starting Over

Firehouse Blues Series: Book 4

AE Moran

Invisible Publishing Company

Firehouse Blues Series

Book 1: On Fire

Book 2: Rescue Me

Book 3: Burned Out

Book 4: Starting Over

Book 5: Haunted Past

Book 6: Fallen Hero

Book 7: Fire Chief

Book 8: New Hire

Book 9: Forgotten Love

Book 10: Second Chance

Contents

Chapter 1: Chris   1

Chapter 2: Josh   15

Chapter 3: Josh   25

Chapter 4: Chris   37

Chapter 5: Chris   43

Chapter 6: Chris   53

Chapter 7: Josh   63

Chapter 8: Chris   71

Chapter 9: Josh   81

Chapter 10: Chris   89

Chapter 11: Josh   101

Chapter 12: Josh   109

Chapter 13: Chris   117

Chapter 14: Chris   127

Chapter 15: Josh   141

Chapter 16: Josh   149

Chapter 17: Chris   161

Chapter 18: Josh   169

Chapter 19: Chris   179

Keep Reading   193

Get All of AE Moran's Free Books   195

About AE Moran   197

Also by AE Moran (so far)   199

Chapter 1: Chris

"**M**ission impossible—Staff Meeting Edition," Ellis Barrett jokes.

"Strap in for some extreme managerial torture," Danny Brewer chimes in. "Prepare to have your head squeezed in a vise and your brains squished out through your ears."

Laughter breaks out in the training room as all the firefighters and paramedics of the Howe County Fire Department take their seats.

I sit down between Leila Cunningham and Naomi McPhee. "So which episode of Mission Impossible—Staff Meeting Edition are we up to?" I ask. "Is this episode four hundred and eighty-seven or four hundred and eighty-eight?"

"This is Fry-Your-Brain-In-Paperwork, Episode eight hundred and a thousand," Caleb Watts replies.

"It doesn't work that way, pal," Sophie McNish chimes in. "I think you mean a thousand and eight hundred."

"No, what I actually meant was....."

Fire Chief John Brewer strolls into the room just then. "Okay, cool it, all of you. I have a few quick announcements and then we can proceed to the main gladiatorial event."

"Yes!" Billy Cates pumps his fist. "Now that's the kind of staff meeting I can get on board with."

"Did you bring some lions, tigers, and wild bears for us to fight?" Jessie Nash asks.

"You can fight me, sweetie," Ellis tells her. "I'll be your teddy bear."

The room erupts in laughter again and Billy throws a crumpled-up piece of paper at him. It bounces off Ellis's skull and goes flying. "Give it a rest, Romeo. You're supposed to be a professional here."

"Ellis—professional?" Naomi teases. "Who do you think you're fooling."

John raises his voice over the noise. "First of all, I want to introduce your newest EMT trainee." He waves to one side and a beautiful young woman with long curly hair tied in a ponytail walks in. "Meet Emily Montgomery Brewer."

Danny's new wife, Emily, stops next to John, blushes, and raises her hand in a quick wave. "Hi, guys."

"Is this supposed to be some kind of joke?" Keith Brewer calls from the back. "We all already know Emily."

"Then you won't have any problem helping her out and making her feel welcome," John replies. "Emily is starting on the EMS truck today. Chris will be her training officer."

Caleb swats Danny's shoulder. "Why didn't you tell us, fool?"

"'Cuz it was too funny watching to see your faces when you found out," Danny replies.

"Congratulations, Emily," Brooke Elsworth calls out. "You're gonna be great."

"Yeah, Chris will show you the ropes," Naomi adds. "If you need anything, just let us know."

"Thanks, guys." Emily rocks on her heels and beams at everyone. "It's such an honor to work with all of you."

"Just don't listen to anything Ellis says." Caleb leans forward, unfolds his notebook in half, and places it on Ellis's head to form a teepee. It makes him look comic and everyone laughs.

Ellis hams it up by leaning forward with the notebook still there, bends low, and bats his eyelashes extra fast at Emily. "You can come under my umbrella anytime, Emily. We'll take shelter from the rain...
.."

Danny smacks him hard across the shoulder. "Hey! That's my wife you're talking to!"

Ellis takes the notebook off his head and hands it to Danny. "Here, then. You wear it."

Everyone laughs again, including Emily. Danny swats the notebook back at Ellis.

"If we could all pay attention to the business at hand!" John calls out. "The sooner we get through this meeting, the sooner you can all go back to work. Our next item on the agenda....."

Right at that moment, the alarm rings through the firehouse. People call out jokes to John about escaping his latest form of meeting torture and we all pour out of the room to the garage.

I spot Emily heading for the wrong ambulance and I grab her hand. "Over here!"

"Sorry!" she calls.

"You don't have to apologize," I tell her. "You'll figure it out. Do you want to drive?"

Her face goes white as a sheet and she gulps. "Um...."

"Fine. I'll drive." I hope in the driver's seat. "You can direct me."

"Um....what?" she stammers.

"Just get in!" I tell her. "We gotta go!"

She jumps into the passenger seat and then screams when I turn on the sirens.

"Calm down!" I yell over the noise. "You'll get used to it! Pull up the directions on the computer—there!"

I point to the computer terminal on the ambulance dashboard. I don't really need her to tell me where to go. I can just follow the rescue truck that Keith is already pulling out in front of me.

She needs to learn, though. She frowns at the screen pushing a bunch of buttons. "How do I work this?"

"You better learn because, if we get a patient, you're going to have to drive us back to the hospital!" I swivel the screen around. "Push that button there to get the location and directions. That button there brings up the call details. Read the dispatch notes and tell me what we're in for."

"Oh, my God!" she exclaims. "It's a three-car accident on the highway with multiple casualties!"

I grin at her. "Perfect for your first call-out!"

She gapes at me in horror. I can't help but laugh at her expression. She's really diving into the deep end today.

"Don't worry about it!" I tell her again. "The guys will secure the scene before we even get there. Leila will see any patients first. Then you and I will transport. Got it?"

"But if there are multiple patients....won't we have to treat them, too?"

"Sure! That's what we're here for." I laugh at her expression. "This is what you signed up for! Enjoy it!"

She looks out at the road. The two firetrucks drive in front of us clearing traffic. The second ambulance with Brooke and Naomi follows me and Emily.

I shouldn't make fun of her. It's been so long since I first started doing emergency work. I've long since forgotten the terror of my first day.

The two trucks swing out onto the highway. It doesn't take us long to find the wreck.

The Police have diverted traffic. We have the place to ourselves. Keith parks the rescue truck and he, Leila, and the guys unload in their turnouts.

I grab my drug box and hand Emily the jump kit. "Stick with me. You'll be fine."

She nods fast just as a Police officer comes up to me. "We got three cars all with casualties in them. That one over there is the most serious."

He points to a passenger car flipped onto its roof. The guys stride over to it, but we all see right away that this isn't a normal car accident.

Someone has braced the car with wooden blocks under the roof to stop the vehicle from rocking back and forth or moving around in any other way.

A passenger lies across the front windshield and a different guy lies across the dashboard holding the passenger by the head.

"What the hell?!" Keith growls.

"That guy got here before we did," the officer tells us. "He says he's a paramedic and he stabilized all three cars before we even showed up. He says he triaged all the patients and that man had airway obstruction. He says he had to crawl into the car to hold the guy's airway open until you got here."

"Holy shit!" Leila breathes. "Talk about saving the day!"

Keith waves to everyone. "Spread out and stabilize all the other cars. Leila, go through the scene and double-check the guy's triage. Chris and Emily, you go see what the guy needs and start extricating the patient. Caleb and Billy can help you."

We all split up and I approach the car. The only way to get near the patient is to lie down in front of the windshield, which puts me directly underneath the engine compartment.

Whoever this random civilian is, he sure has blocked the car well—which makes sense. He wouldn't want to crawl inside the car without blocking it.

I double-check the blocks before I stretch out in front of the shattered windshield. "What do we got here?"

"Middle-aged male. His face struck the steering column," the mystery guy tells me. "His pulse was rapid and thready when I got here with unilateral pupil dilation and pink frothy sputum coming from his mouth. His pulse has stabilized since I've been holding his airway open, but he hasn't regained consciousness. He probably has a cerebral injury."

I glance at the patient and then take a longer, closer look at the mystery man. He's a youngish guy with soft, curly brown hair clipped close to his head and big, soft, brown puppy-dog eyes.

Those eyes study me back just as hard. His shoulders bulge with rounded muscles where he holds his arms up to immobilize the patient's head. Whoever this mystery stranger is, he must have been holding the guy's head for a long time. He saved this guy's life.

That's when I notice the mystery stranger wearing a dark blue T-shirt with a Fire Department logo on it—but of course it isn't the Howe County Fire Department logo. This guy doesn't belong to the Howe County Fire Department. I've never seen this guy before.

The logo is from Masterson Fire Department. Masterson is the next big city closest to Howe. If this guy works for Masterson Fire Department, that explains why he's so skilled. So what is he doing saving the day in Howe?

I turn back to the patient, pry open one of his eyelids, and see the pupil dilation the mystery man just told me about. I should ask the guy's name, but the patient is too serious.

"Emily—get that jump kit open. Give us a cervical collar and get this guy on high-flow oxygen right away."

Emily gets to work. She has to crawl onto the dashboard to fit the collar around the patient's neck. She gets the mystery man's fingers stuck underneath it when she tries to pull the Velcro tight.

"Hold on," he tells her. "Wait for me to get my fingers out first."

"Slow down, Emily," I tell her. "There's a procedure to this. I need to take the patient's head from.....Sorry. What's your name?"

"Josh," he tells me.

"I'm Chris and this is Emily. Today is her first day training as an EMT."

Josh nods at her. "Congratulations."

She turns bright red. "Thanks."

"I'll take the patient's head while you put the collar behind his neck," I go on. "When Josh gets the collar in position, he'll take the patient's head again and you can secure the collar in front. Okay?"

She nods fast. "Sorry."

"Stop apologizing," I tell her. "You didn't know."

We get busy on the collar, and while she negotiates with Josh to fit the collar, I pull out the oxygen mask and put that over the patient's head, too.

Then it's my turn. Josh and I talk back and forth until he takes the patient's head again. Just then, Caleb and Billy show up with a backboard and a bunch of restraint straps.

"How do you want to do this?" Billy asks.

I glance at Josh. His eyes are so big and soft and deep that I have to stop myself from looking at him for too long. He sure is hot—and he sure knows his way around a car accident.

He doesn't wait for me to respond. He starts giving orders to the other guys right away. "Clear the broken glass out of the driver's compartment there and put the backboard in here. When I say, we'll rotate him onto the board while he's still in here, secure him, and then you can pull the board out with him on it."

Billy nods. "You got it. Do you want the KED board first?"

"That will just waste time and we would have to move him to get the KED around him. Put the board in here...." Josh glances at me. "As long as you're done."

"Go for it," I tell him.

Billy and Caleb slide the board in. "Get in the car, Chris," Josh tells me. "Rotate his legs onto the board while I turn his head." I get into position. "On three—one....two....three...."

I pull the patient's legs onto the backboard while Billy lifts his hips. Josh rotates the guy's neck perfectly to keep his spine in a straight line. He has definitely done this before—a lot. He has a lot of experience—as much as anyone on the Howe crew.

He calls three more moves before we get the patient into the right position. Then Josh coordinates the whole procedure of removing the board so that he doesn't have to let go of the guy's head while Josh climbs out of the car.

By this time, Caleb and Emily have come over with a gurney. We slide the backboard onto the gurney and secure the guy in place.

I place foam blocks on either side of the patient's head. I have to discuss everything with Josh before he can take his hands away. Then we strap the patient down so he won't move.

I see myself moving extra close to Josh while we work. Everything we do blends into a seamless flow. It almost feels like we've been working together for years. I've only ever felt this with the people who are already on our crew.

The instant Josh takes his hands away, he attacks my drug box like he owns it, pulls out the laryngoscope and an ET tube, tears off the guy's oxygen mask, and starts intubating the patient like nobody's business.

"Give me some suction here, Emily," he orders. "Do you have norepinephrine on board yet, Chris?"

"I'm pushing it now," I tell him as I inject the dose into the patient's IV line.

Emily fumbles with the suction device and accidentally drops it on the ground. "Sorry!"

"Here, let me do it," I tell her. "Help Caleb load the gurney into the ambulance and then you're going to drive us to the hospital. Got it?"

Her eyes fall out of their sockets. "Um...."

"You can do this," I tell her. "You know your way to the hospital from here, don't you?"

"Um.....yeah....." she stammers.

"Then you can drive us there. Go on. Get going." She starts to walk away. "Hey! Take the gurney with you, sweetie."

She comes racing back. I catch Josh smirking at me behind her back on the way to the ambulance.

I suction the patient for him and then he fits the ventilator bag to the ET tube. He squeezes the bag to ventilate the patient in between taping the tube in place. Damn! This guy really knows his stuff.

Josh and I work over the patient while Caleb, Billy, and Emily wheel the gurney to the ambulance. They load it and Josh climbs into the back with me. He doesn't ask permission. He just does it.

He's working too fast to stop now and the guys slam the doors to shut us in. Emily gets into the driver's seat.

"Nice and easy!" I call up to her. "Remember we're working back here."

"Um....okay...." Her voice trembles.

"You can do it!" I tell her. "This guy needs the hospital and you're going to take him there."

"Right," she mutters and puts the ambulance into gear.

I can't keep an eye on her. Josh and I keep working on the patient all the way to the hospital.

He's been in charge this whole time and he stays in charge while he ventilates the patient. He squeezes the bag with one hand, does a million other tasks with his other hand including suctioning, monitoring the patient's vitals, and checking pupil dilation and response every time I give him drugs.

Josh gives me orders in a rapid-fire barrage unlike anything I've ever seen or heard. I feel totally comfortably letting this guy make decisions about my patient's care.

He cranes his head forward and calls to Emily. "Get me the hospital ED staff on the radio. I need to give them a report on our patient before we get there."

"How do I do that?" she yells back.

"I'll show you," I tell her and stick my head up to the cab. I point out the right combination of controls on the computer terminal and hand Josh the microphone.

He rattles off a long list of details, vital signs, drugs and other treatments we've administered, and finally peers through the front windshield to give the medical team our ETA. I've never been more impressed with another paramedic's work.

Before I know it, the ambulance's reversing alarm starts going off. I glance through the back window. "We're there."

She backs up to the loading dock and the medical team opens the doors to unload the patient. Josh stays by the guy's head squeezing away on the ventilator bag while he repeats all the patient details to the team.

Emily and I get shunted to the side while Josh gets swept into the ED. The medical team takes the patient upstairs to surgery, but before we can move, Leila, Sophie, and Naomi come in with another patient.

I pull Emily out of the way and we start restocking our ambulance. "You did great," I tell her.

She turns bright red and looks away. "I was all thumbs. You guys are so much better than I am."

"We have a lot more experience than you do. You sure drove well. You didn't jostle us once."

She squirms. "Thanks."

"You'll get used to it. Come on. Let's get our stuff and check in with dispatch. They might need us to go back out there and bring in another patient."

Emily and I are just coming out of the hospital supply room when we meet up with Keith, Danny, Leila, Sophie, Naomi, Billy, Caleb, and Ellis coming out of the ED.

"What's the situation?" I ask Keith. "Do we need to go back for any other patients?"

"They were all walking wounded," he tells me. "They're self-transporting. We're done."

Leila looks around. "Where's the Caped Crusader?"

"I'm not sure," I reply. "He had to go into the back to ventilate the patient while the medical team took him to surgery. I haven't seen Josh since."

"Josh?" Billy asks. "Is that all you got out of him? Who is he?"

"I didn't have time to give him a personal interview," I counter. "He was wearing a Masterson Fire Department T-shirt, though."

"He sure knew the ropes," Caleb remarks. "He didn't miss a beat."

"He's not bad-looking, either, is he?" Leila chimes in and she elbows me. "You two sure worked well."

"You better watch it," I tell her. "Your husband will get jealous if he hears you talking like that about another man."

"I won't get jealous because every guy is better looking than I am," Keith growls.

"They are not!" Leila puts her arm around him and kisses him on the cheek. "You're the most gorgeous man in the world to me."

Danny bends over and makes a puking noise at the floor. "Gross!"

"Get a room, you two," Caleb tells Keith and Leila.

The others laugh and we all head back outside. Emily and I load up in the ambulance and I make her drive us to the firehouse.

She takes at least five tries to back the ambulance into the garage. I stand behind the unit directing her and waving her in.

Some of the others laugh at her and she turns red again when she gets out and they burst into cheers.

"Leave her alone!" Danny puts his arm around her and kisses her on the cheek. "You did great."

"Get a room!" Keith yells out and more people laugh.

"Come on, Emily," I tell her. "We need to finish our paperwork and then I'll show you how to do a full equipment check on the ambulance."

She follows me and we all turn toward the stairs leading up to the breakroom.

We stop dead in our tracks when we see John standing at the base of the stairs talking to someone. It's a man in a Fire Department T-shirt.

I would recognize that curly brown hair and those soft brown eyes anywhere. It's Josh.

"Holy crap!" Keith mutters. "It's Batman!"

John turns around and frowns at us. "What?"

"He was at the call just now," Caleb replies. "He helped us load the patients."

"He did a lot more than that," I chime in. "He secured the scene, triaged the patients, and saved one of their lives."

"So I hear." John waves at Josh. "This is Josh Abbott. He's going to be starting work here tomorrow morning. He's going to be our new paramedic to fill Ellen's old place."

Chapter 2: Josh

I walk into the garage at the Howe County Firehouse and immediately spot the woman I worked with at the car accident scene yesterday. She stands next to the ambulance talking to the same EMT trainee.

Chris isn't the tallest or the shortest member of the crew, but she's hands down the prettiest paramedic I've ever laid eyes on. She wears her silky black hair in a bob cut to jaw-length. The long front bangs curve inward to frame her face.

She has dimples, too, and her sparkling blue eyes flash with light when she laughs at something Emily says. Damn, Chris is beautiful!

She takes care of herself, too. Her uniform actually shows off how toned and tight her body is instead of making her look dumpy and blocky. The Fire Department uniform doesn't usually do women any favors, but it can't hide her beautiful curves.

I got an eyeful at the accident yesterday, but I'm not here to admire the scenery. I turn off toward the locker room and see the rest of the crew gathering around all the other trucks and ambulances.

Almost everyone present stops what they're doing to watch me cross the garage to the locker room. They all acted so easy-going and down-to-earth yesterday. Now the temperature drops by twenty degrees the minute I walk in.

I put my gear in the locker Chief Brewer assigned to me. I brought a padlock to put on my locker, but I change my mind when I see that none of the other lockers are actually locked. People around here must really trust each other.

That's lightyears different from what I'm used to at Masterson Fire Department. That's just one more thing I'm going to have to get used to around here.

I head back out to the garage and stop by the notice board to check the schedule to see which vehicle crew I'm assigned to today. I'm on the rescue truck and my heart skips a beat when I see that I'm paired with Chris as my partner.

I turn around to find everyone staring at me. They all seem to have gathered between me and the truck.

I brace myself for the whole first-day-of-work onslaught, but I make sure to keep it casual. "Hey, guys," I begin. "It looks like I'm with you today."

"So what's your story, man?" one big, burly guy demands. I think I heard the others calling him Billy.

"What do you mean?" I ask. "I'm starting work here. I'm on the rescue truck working with Chris." I frown at them all. "Didn't Chief Brewer tell you that? Is there a problem?"

"You're the problem, pal," a short, stocky guy with dark brown hair fires back. "Who are you, where do you come from, and how do we know you're any good for this crew?"

I start to open my mouth to answer. This is so not the reception I was expecting.

Before I can say anything, Chris comes over. "Leave him alone, guys. You weren't there yesterday. Josh is perfectly qualified. We all saw that." She turns to me. "You'll have to excuse them. We've had more than twenty different people come through here in the last year. The woman they were supposed to replace was our dear friend and she got injured on a call."

"I'm sorry to hear that," I reply.

"Anyway, we've had one nightmare after another trying to find someone to replace her."

"You got some pretty big shoes to fill," Billy calls out. He has longish, sandy-blonde hair and a scruff of five o'clock-shadow covering his face.

"If you fill them at all," the short guy adds.

"Stop it, George," Chris snaps. "Give him a chance."

Just then, another bunch of people come downstairs from the breakroom. One of them is the rough, scarred biker guy from yesterday's call. Another is a fresh-faced younger dude with dark hair. The third is another woman paramedic.

"Hey, look who's here! It's Clark Kent," the young guy calls. "Hey, champ! You forgot your cape." He holds out his hand to shake mine.

"What are you talking about?" I ask.

"It's a joke about how you saved the world yesterday," the biker guy tells me. "Be prepared to wear that label for the rest of your natural life." He holds out his hand. "Keith Brewer. Welcome aboard."

"Josh Abbott," I tell him. "Thanks."

He bursts out in deep, gruff laughter. "I know that, pal. John introduced you yesterday, remember?"

"Yeah, I remember. So you're a Brewer, too, huh? What—are you his brother?"

"Unfortunately." Keith laughs again. "Never work anywhere with your brother as your boss. This here is our younger brother, Danny." He points out the young guy. "And this is my wife, Leila."

I nod at her. "Nice to meet you."

"You knocked us all dead yesterday," she replies. "You're gonna fit right in here."

I glance at the guys behind me—the ones that suggested I *wouldn't* fit right in here. "Um....thanks."

"What are you rolling out the red carpet for this guy for?" George cuts in. "He could go the way of the dodo bird just like all the others."

"Who cares?" Keith fires back. "He sure knows his stuff."

"Which explains why John hired him," Chris adds.

"John would have hired him based on yesterday's call alone," Danny chimes in. "This dude is a walking, talking....." He trails off and some of the others laugh.

"Yeeeessss?!" Keith asks. "He's a walking, talking what? What were you just about to say? No, don't tell me. Let me guess."

I catch Chris grinning at me, but when I make eye contact with her, she looks away. I think I'm gonna die, she's so beautiful.

Just then, Chief Brewer comes downstairs and sees us all standing around doing a whole lot of nothing.

I sized that guy up the very first time I met him. He's no-nonsense, straight-shooting, and takes no shit from anyone. He's exactly the kind of fire chief I love working for.

He casts a flinty glance around the group. "Is there some reason why none of you is doing your start-of-shift truck checks?"

"Yeah. Certain people got certain ideas about the new guy...." Keith begins, but just then, the alarm goes off.

"You're with me, new guy," Chris tells me, cracks a crazy grin, and hops into the rescue truck's back seat.

I can tell right now I'm going to have my hands full working with this woman.

I jump into the back next to her. She's already shimmying into her turnouts when Keith and Billy scramble into the front. Danny,

George, and another guy who I think is named Caleb get into the middle seat.

The siren blasts through the garage and Keith pulls the truck out onto the road. "What's the call?!" he yells to Billy over the noise.

Billy gets to work on the computer to read the dispatch notes. "Two-alarm fire! Five people inside.....no, the details are coming through now. Four of them are out of the building. Only one left inside." He relays the address to Keith.

I pull up my turnouts, put my suspenders over my shoulders, and stick my arms into my jacket sleeves. "Where's your trainee?!" I yell over to Chris.

"Still on the ambulance!" she yells back. "She has some growing to do before she rides in the truck."

"Why aren't you on the ambulance?" I ask.

"I usually work with Naomi on the ladder truck crew. Leila works the rescue truck...."

"Why isn't she here, then?"

"John's wife, Ellen, was the paramedic on the rescue truck before—the one who got hurt—the one you're supposed to replace. She and Leila were partners for ages. Then Ellen had to leave and we haven't been able to replace her."

"We still haven't," George fires over his shoulder.

Chris makes a face and turns back to me. "Anyway, we've had to rotate to cover the truck since we didn't have a second paramedic. Leila has today off and you're here, so here I am."

I frown at her. "That makes no sense. If you usually work on the ladder truck, why were you on the ambulance yesterday?"

She waves my question away. "The roster has been a horror show since Ellen quit. Poor John has to scramble every month to fill every shift."

"That sucks," I remark.

"Which is why everyone has their panties in such a twist about replacing Ellen," Danny calls over the seat back.

"And why everyone has their panties in a twist about so many people not working out," Caleb adds. "Certain people have started to think the job is cursed."

"Got it," I reply. I'm starting to get a picture of why certain people reacted the way they did when I showed up to take Ellen's place.

"Heads up!" Keith calls back. "Here we go, people! Suit up to rock and roll!"

I stick on my helmet and buckle it while he pulls the truck into the driveway. The fire is nowhere near a two-alarm and we see all five of the residents standing off to one side surrounded by Police officers. It looks like everyone got out by themselves.

We tumble out and Chris and I go over to the escaped residents. "Is anyone hurt?" she asks the nearest cop.

"Naw," he replies. "Just a few bumps and bruises from trying to climb out the windows. This little guy fell out the window and twisted his ankle."

He waves at an eight-year-old boy. His mother keeps her arm around his shoulders.

Chris waves everyone away from the fire. The crew is already pulling out their hoses to put out the blaze.

"Everybody come over here and we'll check you out to make sure you don't have any more serious injuries," Chris tells the patients and turns to me. "Let's split them up. I'll take the mother and son. You take the other three."

"Where are we going to stay tonight?" the mother asks in a shaky voice. "What are we going to do?"

"Let's get you checked out first," Chris replies. "You can worry about that afterward. If it all goes well, none of you has to spend the night in the hospital."

That seals the deal. She leads the mother and son to the ambulance that Emily and one of the other paramedics pulls up onto the curb. I lead the other three patients over there, too.

Chris sits the mother and son on the gurney. I tell everyone else to sit on the bumper.

One of the patients is the boy's middle-aged father. Another is a grandmotherly type and the third is a teenage girl with heavy black eye makeup. She looks like the boy's older sister.

I start with the old lady, ask her the usual round of questions, and start taking vitals and doing an exam. None of these people looks like they're in any distress at all.

Chris is working on the boy and I finish with the old lady. I turn to the girl. "Did you get hurt getting out of the house? Do you have any pain anywhere or in your lungs?"

She gives me a dirty look, but right then, Caleb comes racing over to us. "You guys gotta come quick. There were three homeless guys camped out in the shed behind the house. We didn't find them until right now. They're really bad! You guys gotta come right away."

I snatch the jump kit from the back of the ambulance. Chris and I leave our patients sitting there and hustle to the back of the house.

The other firefighters are still hosing down the fire, but it doesn't seem to be getting any smaller.

We head for the backyard and my heart sinks. The shed is attached to the house. The whole house wall has been burned to a cinder and the shed roof is nothing but a mass of black. Most of the shed has been charred black, too.

The guys on the fire crew have left the shed door open and it's pitch dark inside. I switch on my flashlight, and before I even look inside, I know it's bad.

The three homeless guys lie top to tail on the shed floor. They must have been sound asleep when the house went up. They still have their eyes closed and they're burned all over their bodies.

Most of their clothes have been burned off, but I can't see any skin underneath because it's all a mass of third-degree burns.

"Jesus!" Chris husks. Then she bellows through the door. "Get Emily and Naomi over here NOW!! And get every gurney and backboard we have! We gotta transport these guys on the double!"

I kneel down next to first guy closest to the door. The shed is so cramped that I barely have room to open the jump kit.

I check the first guy. "He's still breathing, but barely."

"This one, too." Chris squats next to the guy on the far side. Neither of us can get any closer to the guy in the middle.

I lean over and rest my gloved hand on the middle guy's chest. "He's breathing."

I tear into the kit and pull out an oxygen mask for the first guy. I'm busy fitting it to his face when Naomi, the other paramedic, sticks her head in. "What do we got?"

"You won't be able to fit in here," I tell her. "Get the extrication equipment so we can get these guys out."

She tries to step inside anyway and trips over my patient's feet. "Woops!"

"Get out!" I tell her. "I told you there's no room."

She stumbles and almost pitches across the patients before she blunders outside again. I get back to work, and a second later, Danny shows up with a backboard.

He can't fit in here, either. He balances on the doorstep and helps me load the patient on. We have to be extra careful and add bandaging and non-stick film under the straps so they don't stick to the patient's burns.

We finally slide the first patient out. Naomi and Emily stand there waiting. "Take this one while we get the other two out."

I don't stick around to wait. Danny and I get busy loading up patient number two. We can work better, now that we have more space.

I take a set of vitals on the patient. "How's it looking, Doc?" Danny jokes.

"He's in shock—probably because his lungs are burned. He has to go." I boost the patient's oxygen supply and we bust our asses getting the patient out of the shed.

Chris has been working non-stop on patient number three. By the time Danny and I get there, she has him intubated and is pumping him full of drugs through his IV.

She has to work one-handed so she can ventilate him while she works. "Let's get another firefighter in here to extricate this guy!" I yell through the door. "I gotta help Chris."

Caleb comes in. I get busy helping Chris clear the guy's airway and giving the guy another round of drugs while Caleb and Danny load the guy onto a backboard.

We're just about to lift him off when the EKG attached to the guy's chest squeals with an alarm. "He's crashing!" Chris yells and raises her voice to bellow out into the night. "We need another pair of hands here! Caleb—start compressions!"

I jump on the drug box. "I'm giving him another dose of epi and vasopressin!"

"Stand clear to defibrillate!"

We both go into a seamless flow of calling and working together exactly the way we did yesterday. I don't have to question anything she does. She's already thinking it before I say a word.

Caleb starts doing compressions on the patient. Billy comes in and he and Danny carry the backboard outside. They put the patient on a gurney while me, Chris, and Caleb work nonstop to keep the guy alive.

Chapter 3: Josh

The other firefighters wheel the gurney out to a waiting ambulance. Naomi and Emily are long gone. We get into the back with a male paramedic and a male EMT.

The EMT starts driving us to the hospital, but Chris, Caleb, and I don't notice. "Clear!" Chris yells.

Caleb and I both take our hands off the patient while she defibrillates him. Then we all get to work just as fast. Sweat pours down Caleb's face.

I jerk my chin at the other paramedic—the one who was on the ambulance crew when Chris and I loaded on with our patient.

The other paramedic has been sitting aside to keep out of our way. "You take over compressions at the next shock," I tell him.

"Who the hell are you?" he fires back.

"Do it, Andy!" Chris roars. "You can see Caleb is exhausted. You aren't doing shit!"

Andy shuts his mouth in a hurry, and when Chris delivers the next shock, Caleb moves aside and Andy takes over compressions.

It doesn't matter, though, because our EMT driver is already pulling up to the ED. Andy gets away with just doing five minutes of compressions and then the medical team takes the patient off our hands.

I stand in the ED with Caleb and stare after them. This is the hardest part—the part where I have to stand here and not be able to do anything. The patient's life is out of my hands.

Chris turns away and storms off somewhere. I turn to Caleb. "You okay, man?"

He nods and wipes his sweaty forehead across his sleeve. "Thanks, man."

I clap him on the shoulder. "You're a trooper. You did great."

He grins at me and jerks his thumb over his shoulder. "I guess I'll start restocking."

"Sit down and take a break. You deserve it. Let Andy restock."

He laughs. "You're new around here. You'll learn."

I don't know what he means until I finish my paperwork. I'm just about to go help restock the unit when I see Andy standing out on the loading dock shooting the breeze with two nurses.

That shithead better not have been sitting on his ass instead of restocking. I better not find out he was socializing with a couple of girls and letting Caleb do all the work.

That must be what Caleb meant about me being new around here. Andy is one of *those* kinds of paramedics—the kind that lets other people carry the load while he rides on their coattails.

I put my clipboard away and head for the supply room when I meet Caleb coming the other way. He carries a whole armload of IV supplies, ET tubes, saline bags, and piles of bandages.

"Don't worry about it," he tells me. "I got it."

I frown at him. "Where's Chris? Have you seen her?"

His smile evaporates. "I thought she was out there with you."

"I thought she was back here with you," I counter.

We both look around, but Chris isn't here. He leaves to go put the stuff away. I stop by the ED nurses' station. "Have you seen Chris

Daniels?" I ask. "She was with us when we brought in that burn victim."

"She stopped by here ten minutes ago to find out how the patient was," the nurse behind the desk replies. "Then she went off that way."

"How *is* the patient?" I ask. "What's his status?"

"He didn't make it," she murmurs. "He flatlined a few minutes after you brought him in."

I cringe. "Did you tell Chris that?"

The nurse nods and gives me a sympathetic look. Damn it. Now I know why Chris disappeared.

I head off down the hall in the direction she said Chris went. I have to hunt around before I spot her in a janitor's closet halfway down the hall.

She stands with her back to the open door. I step in there behind her. "You okay?" I murmur.

She sniffs and answers over her shoulder without turning around, but I can hear in her voice that she's still crying. "Yeah, I'm fine. Patients like that just get to me, you know?"

"Yeah, I know. Do you want me to call Chief Brewer for you?"

"No!" she snaps. "I'll be all right. What are the others doing?"

"Caleb is restocking the truck and Andy is standing around with his head up his ass."

She bursts out laughing in between choking sobs. "You learn quick for a new guy."

I have to smile at the back of her head. She's pure gold, this one. "I do my best."

She turns around, runs her sleeve across her face, and does her best to smile at me. It isn't her usually brilliant grin, but it's good enough. "Sorry."

"Don't mention it. It happens to the best of us." I nod toward the door. "Are you ready to go?"

"Yeah. Let me stop by the bathroom and wash my face. I'll meet you out on the loading dock."

I nod and leave her alone. I find Caleb in the ambulance stuffing all the supplies into their places. Andy is just saying goodbye to his nurses when I show up.

Andy and his unnamed EMT driver get into the front. I get into the back and start helping Caleb when Chris shows up. She looks normal. No one would ever know anything was wrong.

We ride in the back on our way to the firehouse. "What brought you up here from Masterson?" she asks me on the way.

"Just time to move on," I tell her. "I guess I was ready to leave the big city behind and work in a firehouse where people don't have to put padlocks on their lockers during their shifts."

Her eyes fall out of their sockets. "No way!"

I nod. "Moving here is like moving to another country."

"Damn, dude!" Caleb chimes in. "I was planning on leveling up to Masterson someday. Now you went and spoiled my pipe dream."

"It isn't so bad in other ways," I tell him.

"It can't have been that good if you left," Chris exclaims.

"It's a big city. I wanted something a little more comfortable—maybe somewhere where everybody knows their neighbors and treats each other that way."

"Hey, we're having a firehouse barbecue on Saturday," she tells me. "You should come."

My head shoots up. "Really?"

"Definitely. The firehouse is one big family. We have barbecues or pool night or something every other week just to hang out and bond. You should come."

"That would be great. Thanks."

"You wouldn't sound so surprised if you knew how many losers have tried and failed to fill Ellen's position. If they've been invited to the barbecue, you definitely need to be."

I glance over at Caleb, but he only nods. "I hope you like your steaks well done," he informs me. "The Brewer boys have a thing about fire."

I laugh. "Now I'm scared."

They both laugh, too, and the mood lightens considerably was our anonymous EMT driver backs the ambulance into the firehouse garage. The trucks and the other ambulance are already in there.

We get out to finish straightening our equipment. We put everything away and head for the stairs to go up to the breakroom.

Chris, Caleb, and I run into a bunch of people blocking our way. "What are you doing inviting this guy to the barbecue on his very first day of work?" Andy demands. "Didn't you even think to check with us first?"

Chris jolts back like he slapped her. "Check with you first?! Are you stupid? Josh works here now. He's as entitled to go to the barbecue as anyone."

"It's his first day," George interrupts. "Today could be his last day."

"Then you won't have to worry about him coming to the barbecue, will you?" she fires back.

"You should have at least asked us," Billy counters. "We don't even know this guy."

"He was shooting orders around like he's the king of the world on that call," Naomi adds. "You got some nerve, pal."

I open my mouth to argue back, but Chris cuts me off. "I heard every word he said on that call. He didn't say or do anything that wasn't perfectly professional—and before you start going off about him telling you to get out of the shed, he told you not to come in there in the first place. You stepped on a critical patient because you didn't listen to him."

"That still doesn't give him the right to order us around," Andy interjects. "He's just a paramedic like the rest of us."

"Actually, he does have the right to order us around once he takes responsibility for a patient's care," Caleb chimes in. "If Leila or Chris or Brooke told one of us what to do regarding a patient's care, we would do it without question. You should give Josh the same respect and consideration. Him being new doesn't change that."

"You weren't doing jack shit on that call anyway, Andy," Chris snaps. "If Josh didn't tell you to pony up and do your job, I would have."

Just then, Keith, Leila, Danny, Emily, and three more of their crew come downstairs. They stop dead in their tracks and Keith scowls when he sees us lined up for the Battle of goddamn Gettysburg. "What's going on?" he booms.

"Chris invited Josh to the barbecue without asking us," George replies.

"Since when does anyone need to ask anyone to invite anyone to barbecue?" he fires back. "Josh is a firehouse employee. Where's the confusion in that?"

"My point exactly," Chris adds.

"We don't even know this dude," Billy counters. "He could be out of our lives by the end of the shift. It's happened before."

"You should have at least waited until we got to know him," Naomi chimes in. "That's all we're saying."

"How the hell are we supposed to get to know him if he doesn't come to the barbecue?" Chris demands. "It's the only place we *can* get to know him."

Before anyone can say anything, Chief Brewer comes downstairs. His features harden exactly like Keith's. Now I see the resemblance.

Chief Brewer keeps it casual and low-key the rest of the time. Now I see where Keith gets his don't-mess-with-me attitude. He learned it from his big brother.

Chief Brewer asks, "What's going on?" in exactly the same tone. He doesn't boom in a deep, gruff rumble. Chief Brewer keeps his voice steady, but I would have to be deaf not to hear that hint of iron creeping in.

Everyone else hears it, too. They all know exactly who they're dealing with when he asks a question like that.

"It appears that certain people didn't want Chris to invite Josh to the barbecue on Saturday," Keith snarls under his breath.

Chief Brewer frowns at our side and then at the other side. "Why do you say she shouldn't have invited him?"

"He isn't part of the firehouse yet," Andy replies. "He's been on a grand total of one call and he...."

"Two calls," Chris interrupts, but Chief Brewer holds up his hand to silence her.

"I seem to recall that the firehouse barbecues and all other firehouse events are open to all firehouse employees, their family members, and even friends they want to bring," Chief Brewer replies. "Did I miss something?"

Keith snorts. "Answer that one, asshole."

Chief Brewer turns around to confront his brother. "Do you mind?"

Everyone on our side shuts their mouths and Chief Brewer turns back to the others. "Well?"

"She should have at least waited until we know if he's going to work out," Naomi points out. "Why should we invest in a total stranger if he's just going to move on in a few days?"

"He will work out," Chris interrupts again.

Chief Brewer doesn't tell her to be quiet again. He stays facing Andy, George, Billy, Naomi, and the others whose names I don't even know.

"All right," Chief Brewer replies. "I'll tell you what. We'll do it your way and I'll revoke Chris's invitation."

"John!" Chris shrieks. "You can't do that!"

"No, man!" Keith counters. "You can't give in to these vultures!"

"Let him come," Leila chimes in. "He earned it yesterday and we've invited people who aren't related to the firehouse before. He should come. What better way to make him welcome?"

Chief Brewer turns around with exaggerated slowness. "I'm handling this, not you." He waits for them to shut up again. I feel sick. I really want to leave. Today couldn't have gone worse.

He faces the other side again. "Well? I'm revoking Chris's invitation. Does that satisfy you?"

They exchange glances and Naomi nods. "Yes. Thank you. That's all we asked."

"Good. That's settled, then." Chief Brewer turns back around and faces me. "We're having a barbecue on Saturday, man. You should come. We'd all like to hang out with you in a non-work environment and get to know you. What do you say?"

I burst into a huge grin. "I'd love to. Thanks."

Chris and all the others on our side explode with laughter, hold their sides, and point at their crewmates. "Ha ha!!" they all cheer.

"Suck on it, assholes!" Danny hollers.

Chris lunges for Chief Brewer and gives him a massive hug. "You're the best, John!"

He grins down at her. She's glowing again.

He smiles at me over her head. "See you Saturday. Leila is one of the organizers. She can give you directions if you need them."

He walks off to the stairs and Chris shoots the finger at everyone on the other side of the confrontation. "It looks like you're all gonna be getting to know Josh in a non-work environment on Saturday. See you there."

She smirks at me and heads back to the supply cabinets to finish her work.

I keep myself busy so I won't see the others glaring at me. I didn't intend to turn my first day of work into a standoff. It looks like I walked into a hornet's nest of conflicting emotions here.

I wait what I hope will be an appropriate amount of time and then get the start-of-shift checklist for the rescue truck. I don't know if anyone else has done it yet, but I want to familiarize myself with the truck while we have some downtime.

I'm sitting in the back seat going through the paramedics' jump kit when Chris sticks her head through the door. "You're a slave to the grind, aren't you?" she teases.

I shoot a look past her toward the stairs. The rest of the crew is up in the breakroom laughing and having a blast. I've been pretending not to hear them since I got into the truck. "I don't think going upstairs is a very good idea right now."

"I don't blame you." She climbs into the seat next to me and cracks open the drug box. "Do you want some help?"

I look down at my clipboard. "Sure. Thanks."

She starts reading the labels on the drug ampules. "We should have restocked on epi at the hospital."

"That's my fault," I tell her. "Caleb was restocking and he doesn't have access to the drug stores. I should have done it."

She smiles at me from under her long black bangs. Those eyes give me butterflies. "It was my fault, too. I shouldn't have let my feelings stop me from doing the job."

"No way," I tell her. "You can't help it when a patient gets to you. It happens."

"Hold the fort. I'll get it from the firehouse supply." She leaves and comes back a minute later with the drugs. "There. Now we're all set."

I check it off on the clipboard. She checks the vasopressin next. "We both forgot to get that, too," she remarks. "Don't tell anyone. We're batting oh-for-two."

"Hey, Chris?" I blurt out.

She looks up. "Yeah?"

"Thanks for backing me up—always. I really appreciate it. I....I didn't think my first day would go like this."

She winces. "I'm really sorry about the way everyone is acting—I mean, not everyone. I'm really sorry you have to deal with this. It isn't fair. It's just.....you wouldn't believe the people we've had come through here. It's been a nightmare with the schedule and everything. Everyone is on edge about finding a replacement for Ellen and it's been going so badly for so long—it isn't personal. Hey, everyone who was on the call yesterday saw how you are. The others will come around. Just give them a chance—and let them give you a chance. It will work out. You'll see."

I can only mumble, "Thanks." I've never been this grateful to anyone in my life.

She bursts into another one of those magnificent smiles with her eyes sparkling and her beautiful little dimples showing. "I have a really good feeling about you. Leila is right. You're going to fit right in here."

She goes back to rummaging in the drug box. I pretend to check off the items as she calls them out, but I can't stop looking at her over the clipboard. I have a good feeling about her, too. I just don't want her to find out about it yet—not until I know where I stand with this job.

Chapter 4: Chris

I huff and puff carrying a loaded cooler down to the beach. I let it fall into the sand and straighten up to stretch my back.

A bunch of firehouse kids are already running around splashing and playing in the waves. Their happy shrieks echo down the beach.

Danny's stepson Zeke runs around with the others. He's part of the pack now. Leila comes up behind me and sets a bunch of grocery bags on the picnic table.

Emily shows up next and their sister-in-law Ellen limps after them. She puts bags of paper plates, cups, napkins, and plastic cutlery down next.

Leila's uniform jacket hides her pregnant belly. She's been getting bigger these last few months, but she still shows up to work every day.

"How much longer are you going to keep working?" I ask her.

"Not much longer," she tells me. "Hey, how would you like to get yourself a full-blown hernia by helping me and Ellen bring the coolers down from the car?"

I grimace. "Don't you have husbands for that?"

They all laugh, but just then, Emily says, "Here comes Josh. We can ask him."

"Ask him what?" Josh asks as he pulls up to the picnic table.

"Oh, hell no!" I interject. "You are not putting him to work. This is his very first barbecue. Give the guy a chance to settle in before you start cracking the whip."

"Ask me what?" he asks again.

"Don't listen to anything they say," I tell him.

"We were just going to ask you....." Leila begins.

"I'll do it!" I blurt out. "I'll carry the damn coolers."

"Oh, is that all?" he asks. "I thought it was going to be something serious. I can carry coolers. Where are they?"

"There's one in my car and one in Leila's," Ellen tells him.

"I'll do it," I repeat. "Stay here, Josh. You're the guest of honor."

He snorts. "Don't try to flirt with me. Which cars are yours?" he asks them.

"I'll show you," I tell him. "At least let me carry one side of the cooler."

He grins at me. "Okay. You're hired."

Ellen steps forward and extends her hand to him. "I'm Ellen, John's wife. It's nice to meet you."

"Oh, I see," he replies. "The big hero."

She frowns. "What?"

"You're the big shoes I'm supposed to fill. You're everyone's favorite paramedic. You're the standard I'm supposed to live up to."

She blushes and grins. "I don't know about that."

"Go on. Admit it," Leila tells her. "The whole firehouse fell apart when you left."

"It did not," Ellen counters. "It's still running perfectly well." She turns to grin at Josh. "Don't listen to her."

"That's what I just told him," I interject and bump my knuckles against his shoulder. "Come on. We're on cooler duty."

We head back to the parking lot where I break into Ellen's trunk. "She seems nice," Josh remarks when we take the cooler out.

"She's great. Losing her was a blow."

"I'm starting to see that. So......Emily....."

"Danny's wife. Howe firehouse is Brewer Central."

He laughs. "Got it. I'll catch up here one day."

"You're fine. Don't worry about it."

We lug the cooler down to the beach and then get Leila's for her. The rest of the crew shows up by the time we get there.

"Yo!" Keith greets Josh and shakes his hand. "Have a beer."

"No, thanks," Josh replies. "I don't drink."

"Oh." Keith frowns and then shrugs. "Well, do you want something non-alcoholic?"

"Uh....okay."

Keith fishes a frosty bottle of sparkling cider out of the cooler. Josh twists off the cap. People start to gather around the way they usually do.

I don't hear anyone making any snide remarks about Josh being here. They wouldn't dare, now that John is the one who invited him.

No one mentions the burn victims, either. If anyone else had been on that call with me, I would have been worried about them making a joke of me getting emotional about it.

Something tells me Josh won't do that. He hasn't mentioned it to anyone since it happened and he was too understanding about it when it did happen. He really does understand. Of course he does. Every paramedic has cases like that.

Billy and Naomi both join our circle. Ellis starts off the festivities without missing a beat. "Did you hear the one about the guy who got his wiener stuck in a beer bottle?"

"We're about to start eating here, man!" Keith booms. "Do you really have to open with that?"

"You really need to upgrade your sense of humor, pal," Caleb tells Ellis. "You're reaching when you start telling jokes like that."

"No, seriously!" Ellis counters. "It was a real patient they got at the ED. One of the nurses told me."

"Actually, he's telling the truth," Ellen chimes in. "I helped treat the patient."

"You didn't tell me about this," John interjects. "Should I be jealous?"

Everyone laughs and she turns bright red. "Okay, I didn't actually treat him. I just saw him from a distance, and trust me, there was nothing to get jealous of."

"Tell us," Danny calls out. "Give us all the gory details."

"NO!!" John snaps.

The others laugh some more, and fortunately, Leila saves us all by turning to Josh. "So you worked at Masterson before this? What brought you up here?"

He shrugs again. "I needed to get out of town and I saw an opening at Howe, so I applied."

My head shoots up. He didn't tell us this in the ambulance.

"Why did you need to get out of town?" Danny asks. "Was it that bad?"

"There was nothing wrong with the firehouse," Josh replies. "I liked it there. It was personal."

A hush falls over the circle. Keith mumbles, "Oh," again. No one asks what the personal thing was. We don't ask those questions.

Josh plows right on ahead as if someone *did* ask him what the personal thing was.

"My partner got killed on duty," he blurts out. "He was my best friend since grade school and we were partners on the fire crew for eight years. A burning timber fell on him during a call and he died right in front of me. I almost died trying to get him out....so things kind of spiraled after that. I was engaged to his sister and his death wrecked her. She broke off our engagement and disappeared out of my life. I've been putting it back together since then, so I guess starting over somewhere else is part of that."

Dead silence answers him. He's been laughing and drinking right along with the rest of us up until now.

He says it so casually like it's all part of the process—which it is.

I can't let him just stand there with that silence hanging over his head. I shoot out a hand and squeeze his arm. "We all know how it is. We lost John's first wife to cancer and then Ellen got hurt....we've all been there—not as bad as your situation, but if you ever need anything, we're here. We're family and you're one of us now. You only have to ask if you need anything."

"Yeah, man," Billy calls out. "That's some messed up shit."

"Thank you for telling us, Josh," Leila exclaims. "We all want to get to know you—the real you. We're all here for you if you need us."

He stares down at the bottle in his hands. "Thanks. I haven't been able to talk about it since it happened—not to anyone who really understands."

"We get it," Danny tells him. "I wish we didn't, but we do."

"Hey, at least you don't have your wiener stuck in a beer bottle, right?" Ellis chimes in. "It could be worse."

Josh laughs and the rest of us join in. "You are such a jackass, Ellis," Keith growls.

"I'm a jackass, but my wiener still works," he replies.

"Can we please stop talking about that?" Ellen asks. "Surely one of you must have another call you want to talk about."

"We had a call for a car accident where a guy got his head stuck through the gap in the steering wheel," Caleb interjects.

"You are so lying!" Leila countered. "I don't believe you."

"I'm not making it up." He points around the circle. "Billy, George, and Drew were there. We had to cut the guy out with the Jaws of Life."

Leila turns to Billy. "Is that true? How could a guy get his head stuck through the gap in a steering wheel?"

"Maybe he was a contortionist," Danny suggests and the circle erupts in laughter.

"Maybe he was on some hallucinogen, momentarily transported to a parallel dimension, and rematerialized with his head through the steering wheel," Josh suggests.

The circle erupts in talk with everyone shooting the wildest comments and fantastical scenarios back and forth. Chaos reigns for a few minutes and then Keith splits away to check the barbecue.

John's daughter Oakleigh comes over to ask him something. He has to bend over to put his ear near her mouth so he can hear her. Then he goes off somewhere to deal with whatever she wants him to deal with.

The barbecue breaks up with different people talking to different people in clusters of ones and twos. I get talking to Sophie McNish. The next time I look, Josh is talking to Billy by the picnic table, so I guess everything is all right now.

I knew he would fit in. That story he told about his dead partner really hit a nerve. Now everyone wants to help him get back on his feet.

That's how it is on the fire crew. When one person stumbles or falls, everyone gathers around to help them get back up again.

Chapter 5: Chris

My sister Lisa drapes her arm over my shoulder and whispers in my ear. "Which one do you want—the tall one or the short one?"

I shrug her arm off. "Neither. I'm not here to cruise."

She laughs and slumps onto her stool. I take my pool cue and bend over the table to take my next shot. Our friends Tina, Veronica, and Amelia sit around on stools behind me. They take turns sipping drinks from their glasses on the counter against the wall.

I sink a few balls until I miss. Then I wander over to my friends and take another pull of my own drink while I wait for Lisa to take her turn.

She misses on the very first stroke and saunters over to me. Her heavily painted lips pout and she scoops her hair sideways so it hangs over her face. "How come you're so good at pool?"

"Try drinking less beforehand," I tell her. "It will improve your aim."

She makes a face. "Where's the fun in that?"

Veronica goes next. She wears an ultra-short skirt and makes no effort at all to hide herself when she bends over the table.

Three guys leer at us from the next table. One of them is a six-foot-five giant with a shock of blonde hair hanging over his eyes.

The dude next to him is much shorter and more powerfully built in the shoulders.

The third guy is somewhere in the middle height-wise. He wears his curly brown hair cut close to his head and he definitely takes care of himself, but his eyes say it all.

They're hard, cold, and mean. Looking into them is like looking at a brick wall. There's nothing behind them—nothing he lets anyone see.

I avoid eye contact with all three guys, but my sister and my friends don't make it easy. Lisa and our friends keep smiling at the guys.

I swear Veronica hits the balls so she has an excuse to shoot from their side of the table. They can probably see straight up her skirt when she bends over.

I dread the moment when the guys decide to make their move and it happens sooner than I expect. All three of them stand up and saunter over to us.

The tall one starts it off. "Good evening, ladies. Can we buy you a round of drinks?"

"We're good, thanks," I tell them.

Lisa sidles over to the tall guy. "That would be awesome. Thank you. Where are you guys from?"

"We're Howe originals, born and raised." The guy thumps his chest like the gorilla he is.

The curly-haired one shoves between Lisa and his big friend, turns his back to his friend, and leers right down into her face. "Who are you going home with tonight, baby? Come home with me. I'll show you a good time."

I pivot off my stool, grab her arm, and tow her away from them. "That wouldn't be a good time unless you want to wind up facing criminal charges in the morning. She's already plastered too far out of her mind to give consent."

She stumbles toward me and almost falls over. I have to catch her to steady her. "Cut it out, Chris!" she tells me. "I'm enjoying myself here!"

"You're enjoying yourself too much." I push her onto her stool.

The short guy comes over to me. "Maybe *you* need to enjoy yourself a little more....Chris."

I snort at him. "I wouldn't be enjoying myself with you. That's for sure."

"What's your problem?" He leans against the counter and grins down at me. "Whatever it is, we can definitely work it out."

I snort again, but Tina distracts him by grabbing his hand and pulling him toward the pool table. "Don't worry about her. She had a bad day at work. Come over here and play a game of pool with me."

He frowns at me and then turns his grin on her. "I will definitely play with you, baby."

She laughs. I turn away to take another sip of my drink.

Lisa downs the rest of hers and stands up. "I'm going to get a refill."

I push her back down. "You've had enough. You aren't going anywhere except home."

"You never let me have any fun," she counters. "You might be incapable of having fun, but that's no reason to stop me."

I look away again. I don't like seeing her like this.

The big guy comes over to me next. "Maybe you need to let your hair down a little bit. What do you think?"

He raises his hand to touch my hair. I move my head away and that's when I see Josh sitting at the bar. He's by himself nursing a drink. It isn't anything alcoholic. He's drinking a Coke.

"Oh, look, there's Josh," I remark to no one in particular.

"Who?" Amelia squints in the direction of the bar.

"That guy." I point him out. "He just started at the firehouse. I'm gonna go talk to him."

Lisa grabs my hand. "Stay here! You don't want to talk to that guy. He's a loser."

"You don't even know him," I tell her.

The tall guy swivels in front of me to block my path to the bar. "He must be a loser if he's alone."

"Why would you go talk to him when you have us to talk to?" the short one interjects.

I roll my eyes to Heaven and swivel around the tall one to walk away. I would have left a long time ago if I wasn't worried about Lisa getting home safely.

These guys only make me more concerned about her. Hooking up with a bunch of idiots like them is exactly the kind of thing she would do.

I start feeling better the minute I get away from those guys. I sashay over to the bar and plop down on the stool next to Josh. "Hi," I tell him.

He brightens up instantly. "Hi. Where did you come from?"

I point across the room. "My sister and our friends are over there playing pool. I saw you, so I decided to come over and say hi. So...hi."

"You said that already." He glances toward the pool tables. "Your friends look busy."

I groan. "Please. So what are you doing here all by yourself? You can drink Coke anywhere, you know. You don't have to go to a bar to do it."

He runs his thumb down the edge of his glass. "I just didn't feel like hanging out at home alone. I guess coming here and drinking alone doesn't help, either."

I get serious when I hear him talking like that. "You should have called me......or someone from the firehouse. I mean....anyway, you know what I mean. We really are here if you need to talk or just want someone to hang out with."

He looks up. "Thanks. If I knew you felt that way, I definitely would have called you."

I blush and look away. "You know what I mean."

"I do know what I mean and I would take any excuse to call you." He swivels toward me on his stool. "So are you seeing anybody?"

I can't stop blushing and I burst into nervous giggles. "No, I'm not seeing anybody."

"Why not? You're gorgeous. Why hasn't one of the firehouse guys asked you out yet?"

I look away. "Let's not go there."

"I'm going there." He leans a little closer. "Come on. You know all my secrets. Tell me yours." He moves his hand across the bar and covers mine. "I want to know everything."

I turn bright red, but when I try to look away again, I get caught by his eyes. He really is hitting on me and he's doing a damn good job of it.

He lowers his voice to a sultry murmur that carries straight into my ear. It cuts through the noise and makes my heart flutter. "You've been so nice to me, Chris."

Just then, the bartender comes over and distracts us. "Can I get you anything?" he asks me.

"Oh, no, thank you," I reply. "I'm done for the night."

"Done?" Josh asks. "You just got here."

"I've been here for an hour and a half already. I don't need to drink any more, especially since I have to drive my sister home."

"Do you want something non-alcoholic?" Josh asks and turns to the bartender. "Give her a Coke on me."

I look up at him and those eyes melt me again. "Thanks."

"It's nothing. Do you want to play some pool?"

"You mean.....?"

He leans a little closer. "I don't want to be alone and I can't think of anyone I'd rather not be alone with than you."

The blood rushes to my cheeks, but fortunately, the bartender comes back right then and puts the glass in front of me. Josh pays for it and picks up the glass. "Come on. Play some pool with me."

He carries the glass to the nearest empty table and puts the glass on the counter against the wall. I stand up and follow him. It looks like we're going to play some pool together.

He pulls some change out of his pocket and starts setting up the table. He grins when he hands me my cue. "Prepare yourself to lose epically."

"Oh, you think so?" I tease. "We'll see about that."

"What—are you a hustler in disguise?" he counters.

"It sounds like *you're* a hustler in disguise. What makes you so sure you'll win?"

"We had a pool table in the breakroom at Masterson firehouse," he tells me. "We played a lot in our downtime."

My smile evaporates. "Oh."

He laughs at me. "There's still time to make a dignified retreat before I wipe the floor with your ass."

I narrow my eyes at him, but I can't help but grin. "You're on. We'll see who wipes the floor with whose ass."

"You can do whatever you want with my ass anytime you want to." He points his cue at the table. "I'll even let you break because I'm a nice guy that way."

I pretend not to notice him making suggestions like that and go to the head of the table. I bend over and break the stack of balls. They roll away in all directions and two colored balls sink.

"Oooooo!" He cringes. "I'm hurt."

I laugh and sink two more balls before I miss. "Read 'em and weep, sonny."

"Now sit down and watch how the experts do it." He moves around the table to its other side. "You're going to need a paramedic when I get through with you."

"I guess it's a good thing there will be one on hand, then," I counter.

He shoots me a grin across the table. "Maybe I can beat you well enough that you'll need mouth to mouth."

I blush and look away. "It's a little early in our professional relationship for that, don't you think?"

"It's never too early for that." He makes his shot and sinks two striped balls right away.

He moves around the table and I realize my mistake when he sinks two more. He's really good—much better than I am.

He sinks his fifth ball and then misses his next shot. He strides over to me and takes a sip of his Coke. "Thanks for hanging out with me."

"Sure," I tell him. "I meant what I said. If you want to hang out with someone, you only have to ask—I mean, not in that way, but if you just don't want to be alone."

He looks away and rubs the dew off his glass. "Thanks. These last couple of months have been a nightmare."

I don't know if he wants to talk about it, but we aren't exactly in the right environment for it.

I decide to change the subject. "Why don't you drink alcohol?"

"The idiot who started the fire that killed my friend was drunk out of his mind. He was holding a drink in one hand and trying to cook with the other. He stumbled and his drink sloshed on the stove. That's how the fire started."

He looks up at me and his eyes somehow become even softer and deeper than I ever imagined. He looks straight into me and I can't look away.

"I guess I felt like.....it was never going to be a good idea to do anything that might reduce my ability to control myself. I guess I felt like anything could happen—anything at all—even if it wasn't something related to me losing control. I guess I kind of decided that it would always be better to stay as in control as possible as much of the time as possible." He shrugs. "That's why I did it. It might not make any sense, but it seemed like the right thing to do at the time."

"It does make sense." I glance over my shoulder at the other table. "I should probably go check on my sister. She was pretty sloshed before."

He nods. "I understand. Have a good evening."

I hesitate. I don't want to just walk away from him. I'd rather hang out with him than Lisa and my friends, especially with those guys hanging around.

I look up to find him studying me with those eyes. What is he thinking? He's been making suggestions ever since I first sat down next to him. Is he thinking about *that*—or something else?

Before I can decide what to do, Lisa, my three friends, and the three guys come over to me. Lisa grabs my hand. "Come on, Chris. Come back to our table. Ditch this guy. You'll have more fun with us."

I pull my hand out of her grasp. "You're having enough fun for both of us. You're shit-faced."

The tallest guy puts his arm around her shoulders to pull her away. "Leave her alone with her loser, baby. We can have fun without her."

She tries half-heartedly to shrug him away. "She's my sister and she needs rescuing from this loser. Come on, Chris. I need you over at your table."

Tina wrinkles her nose at Josh. "Who is this guy, anyway? I've never seen him before. Are you from out of town or something?"

"Yes," Josh replies. He doesn't try to intervene or convince me to stay.

The short guy stalks up to him and shoves him in the chest. "We were talking to this young lady before you interfered. Maybe you should go back where you came from."

"Maybe I should," Josh replies. He takes a step back and bumps into the counter, but he doesn't fight back.

"Stop it." I stand up off my stool and wave the guys and my friends away. "Go back to your table. I'm staying here."

The short guy doesn't stop. He chest-bumps Josh again even though Josh isn't trying to fight back or even argue with him. "This is our town, asshole. You don't come into our town and start stealing girls who don't belong to you."

"Hey—shithead!" I bellow. "I don't belong to you!"

Just then, three security guards come over to us. They try to pull the short guy away from Josh. "Cool it, fellas. If you don't take a step back, you'll have to leave."

"We're leaving anyway," Veronica tells me. "If you want to come with us, you have to come now."

"You're leaving?!" I ask. "Why?"

She slips her arm around the curly-haired guy's waist and grins up at him. "This is why. Some of us know how to have a good time even if you don't."

"You're......" I shake that thought of my head. "Fine. Come on, Lisa. I'll drive you home."

"I'm not going home. I'm going out with Patrick here." She practically falls into the tall guy's arms.

"You can't go out with him," I tell her. "You can barely walk."

"If you don't want to go out with them, you better stay here and drink Coke with your loser boyfriend." She throws her head in the air. "I don't need you babysitting me. I can take care of myself."

She starts to turn away. Patrick puts his arm around her and shoots me a glare like I'm the one trying to hurt her.

I take a step forward to stop her. "Lisa....."

"Leave me alone," she snaps over her shoulder. "I came here to have a good time and I won't let you spoil it."

The others glare at me, too, and they all walk away. Patrick leads Lisa out of the pool hall. The security guards escort them out and the pool hall goes back to its usual buzz of activity.

Chapter 6: Chris

I stare after Lisa and my friends as they disappear out of the pool hall. I really should go get Lisa and stop her from doing whatever it is she's about to do. She's gotten into trouble before and I can see tonight turning into another disaster.

Josh comes up behind me. "Do you want to go get her?"

I slump onto my stool and cover my eyes. "I can't. She's a grown woman. She makes her own decisions."

"Well, do you have your own car here? I can drive you home if you need me to."

I shake my hair out of my eyes. "I have my own car."

"Come on. Let's get out of here." He takes my cue away from me. We're only halfway through the game.

He really is about to leave. He puts the cues away, takes one last sip of his drink, and comes back over to me. His direct brown eyes look straight into mine.

"Thanks," I tell him.

"Forget it. Let's go."

I stand up. He moves his arm behind me to steer me out of the pool hall, but he doesn't touch me.

I see him making all those little gestures like we might actually be together.

I don't let myself think that. I've known the guy for a matter of days. We aren't together and we aren't going to be together.

We head out to the parking lot. "So is she your younger sister or your older sister?" he asks me on the way.

I make another face. "Older sister—but I'm the older sister if you know what I mean. She started going a little wild these last few years. Now we have this dynamic where I take care of her and rein her in."

"That must be hard on you," he remarks.

"Maybe I need someone to take care of me and rein me in," I mumble.

"What does that mean?" he asks. "You seem fine to me. You're the responsible one here."

I snort. "You say that because you don't know me."

He stops by my car and frowns at me. "I don't understand. You're one of the most responsible people I've ever met. You're an outstanding paramedic. You've always conducted yourself perfectly on every call I've seen you on. Who could ask for more than that?"

I squirm and look away. "Never mind. Are you going to be okay? Are you going home or are you going to stay out for a while?"

"I should probably go home. We both have work tomorrow." He cracks a grin at me. "We aren't working together on the rescue truck."

"I know. You're with Leila. That should be interesting."

"Why will it be interesting? She seems nice enough."

"She is. She's very nice." I start to turn away toward my car. "See you tomorrow."

"Chris?" he calls out.

I turn around. "Yeah?"

His eyes bore into me for a second and then he steps in and kisses me. I'm not expecting it and I freeze. Then I feel his lips and kiss him back.

That kiss gets deeper and deeper the longer it goes on. His arm slips behind my back and he pulls me against him. I wrap my arms around his neck.

The minute I do, the energy explodes between us. He straps both his arms around my waist and lifts me against him kissing me hard and fast and deep. He snatches my breath away and my stomach flips as I try to keep up with him.

He pivots backward, falls against my car, and crushes me down on him devouring my mouth in deep, passionate, greedy kisses. His tongue meets mine and I moan in spite of myself.

He puffs out one quick exhalation through his nostrils and a surge of heat rushes to his crotch. His package throbs once against my leg.

That feeling ignites something in me that I thought was long dead. My desire for him blasts off the charts. I want him. I want him right here in the damn parking lot if I can get him.

My hips spasm toward him trying to get to the rock-hard heat under his zipper. His breath catches when I rub against him and his hand slides the rest of the way down to my ass.

He squeezes and pulls me deeper against him. I'm wearing biker shorts under a ruffle skirt and my thighs fall on either side of his leg.

He responds by sticking his knee between my legs and guiding my hips forward to rub against him. Holy shit, I can't stop!

I whine in rising need and he burrows his other hand inside my denim jacket. His fingers clamp around my breast through my T-shirt as his mouth and tongue drive me insane.

I can't stop myself from grinding on his leg, I want him so bad. I haven't felt this in so long.

I shouldn't be making out like this with someone I work with. This is the quickest way to drive him off the crew—or get myself fired.

This aching hunger between my legs won't be denied. He's so hot, and when my eyes drift open, I see him staring at me with those big, soft, brown orbs of his.

Him watching me turns me on even more. I need him to see me. I need him to feel how much I want him.

My eyes swim with maddening, ravenous desire as I ride down on his leg one more time. When my vision focuses enough to meet his gaze, the way he's looking at me sends me reeling over the edge again.

He gives a soft little grunt of appreciation and tightens his grip on my ass. Holy fuck, he's hot!

He darts his hand to the edge of my T-shirt, crawls underneath, and burrows up to my bra. He massages my breast through the cup and makes me whine in ecstasy.

I'm just drifting off into another spinning wave of pleasure when a colossal force rips me off him. I have half a second to see Patrick holding me by my jacket collar before his two friends lunge in.

The middle-sized guy punches Josh square in the face and slams his head back against the car. "Josh!!" I scream, but none of them listens.

The shorter two guys punch Josh again and again, and when he buckles to the ground, they start kicking him.

I try to get back to him to help him, but Patrick yanks me away. "Hey!" I yell. "Let me go!"

He laughs at my pathetic efforts. "Say goodbye to your boyfriend, baby! You're coming with us whether you like it or not."

I twist around in his grasp. "JOSH!!"

I can't even see him behind more cars as Patrick hauls me away. The other two stand between the cars kicking something down on the ground.

"You bastards!!" I shriek and try to attack Patrick, but he hauls off and punches me in the face, too.

I stagger from the blow, but he holds me up by the collar and marches me away. He keeps jerking me by the jacket so I can't even walk straight, but I'm struggling too hard to walk anyway.

I try again and again to kick him, but whenever I try, he hits me again. He punches me in the stomach, and when I still don't stop, he clubs me to the ground with brutal force.

I collapse on the pavement and taste blood. This is bad. I don't know what to do, but I have to get out of this.

I scramble to come up with some way to escape, but before I can move, he grabs me by the hair and yanks me away. "If you want to play rough, we can play rough," he growls. "Have it your own way."

He manhandles me across the parking lot to another car just as the other two catch up. They laugh together. "Your boyfriend won't be coming to save you tonight, honey," the short one gloats. "You are never gonna see that sucker again."

He leers at me and rubs his hands in menacing glee, but Patrick is the one holding me by the hair.

He slams me against the car, pins me under his weight, and starts grinding his body against me while he bites my neck and cheek and ears. "Yeah, baby!" he growls. "You know you're gonna love it."

I burst into a fresh effort of struggling and try to push him off. "Get off me!! Leave me alone!!" I try to kick him again, but he only laughs.

"Come on, baby," he growls. "I saw the way you were doing it with him. You can do it with me, too."

I draw in one huge lungful of air and scream at the top of my lungs. "HELP!! SOMEBODY HELP ME!!"

"Shut the fuck up, bitch!" the curly-haired guy snaps and punches me again. "Shut her up, Patrick. Don't let anyone hear her."

Patrick pulls off me. I try to break away, but he grabs me by the hair again hard enough to make me scream.

He rips me off the car, pulls open the rear passenger door, and hurls me inside. I slam down on the seat and scream again. This can't be happening. I have to find a way to stop this, but he's twice my size and there are three of them.

I spin around just in time to see him standing outside the passenger door. He holds the door open with one hand. He's about to climb into the back seat with me and then I won't be able to do anything to stop him.

These guys will probably drive me somewhere else and then God only knows what will happen.

The other two move around the car. The curly-haired guy takes out his keys and goes through them by the driver's door. He's about to drive the car away with me inside it. The short one goes to the front passenger door.

The whole scene freezes in my mind when I realize what's about to happen. This is my worst nightmare coming true.

Out of nowhere, something flies at Patrick from the side, catches him by the back of the head, and smashes his face into the car doorframe. His head bounces off and I stare in stupid shock at Josh standing there.

Blood covers his face, runs down his neck, and soaks into his shirt. He looks like some kind of monster and his eyes blaze with murderous fury.

He catches Patrick's head a second time, slams it down hard enough to rock the whole car, and lets Patrick's unconscious body fall on the ground. Then Josh turns to the curly-haired driver.

The driver rotates in Josh's direction, but Josh finishes off Patrick so fast that the driver doesn't respond fast enough.

The driver's facial expression goes through a rapid series of changes from determination to terror when he sees the gruesome creature facing him.

Josh hesitates just long enough for the driver to take a good, long look. Then Josh lashes out and strikes the driver in the face. The driver's head whips back.

The short guy races around the car to help his friend. The curly-haired driver recovers from Josh's first punch and swings again, but Josh ducks just as the short guy hustles over.

He charges Josh to close him between both attackers. The curly-haired driver lunges for Josh at the same instant.

Josh sidesteps, and when the short guy passes him, Josh grabs both of them and slams their heads together.

The driver whips back a second time. His eyelids flutter and he buckles on the spot.

The short one takes longer, and when he doesn't fall, Josh seizes him by the head, smashes his face into the car, and the short one goes down, too.

Josh stands over them swaying on unsteady legs. He stares down at the three attackers on the ground, but he doesn't seem to see them. Then, very slowly, he turns around and looks into the car.

I sit frozen on the seat watching the whole thing in stunned amazement. He looks absolutely awful. He did not just kick those guys' asses while he was all beaten up and bloody himself.

He doesn't seem to see me, either. His eyes glaze over and he wobbles. "Josh?" I ask.

He blinks extra slowly and then collapses on the pavement right next to the other guys.

"JOSH!!" I shriek and scramble to get out of the car.

The three attackers are out cold...and so is Josh. I check his pulse and his pupils. He doesn't seem to have a head injury. He just looks terrible with all that blood all over him.

I fumble to get my phone out of my jacket pocket and dial 911 as fast as I can. I can't do anything for Josh like this. I don't even have a BP cuff to find out how badly he's injured.

The emergency operator tells me ambulances are on the way and to wait until they get here. I hang up when I hear sirens. Then I call John Brewer.

The ambulance rolls up and Brooke and Sophie take Josh on board. The rest of the fire crew gets busy transporting the three attackers.

Leila and Drew come over to me after the three ambulances leave. "We need to transport you, too, Chris," Leila tells me.

I look up at her. "Huh? Why?"

"You're bleeding....and you have a black eye. Those guys hit you, didn't they?"

"Um....yeah, but....." I realize a second later that, yes, my face feels puffy and swollen from where those guys hit me.

I let my friends examine me and then they take me to the ED, too. Josh isn't here and none of the attackers are, either.

John rolls in just as the Police show up to take my statement. He stands in the doorway listening to the whole story. I skip the part about how me and Josh were kissing in the parking lot when Patrick attacked us.

As soon as they leave, John sits down on the bed next to me and puts his arm around my shoulders. "You okay?"

I nod down at my hands. "I'm just worried about Josh."

"I'll go check on him after this. You should take a day or two off work just to get your head clear."

"Okay," I mumble.

"You did great." He kisses me on the side of the head. "I'm proud of you."

"He was incredible, John," I croak. "You should have seen him."

He chuckles under his breath. "It sounds like people are gonna be calling him Batman from now on. He'll never get rid of that nickname now."

Chapter 7: Josh

I touch my face and groan. I can barely pick up my head off the pillow, but I don't care because I stopped those guys from attacking Chris. I would do it again.

I shut my eyes and try to block out the incessant throb in my head. How long am I going to be stuck like this?

I'm in a hospital room by myself with an IV hooked up to my arm. I must have gotten beat up worse than I realized.

I really wish I could slip back into a coma, but before I can do that, a nurse comes in to check on me. "How are we feeling this morning?" she asks.

"I don't know about you, but I feel like shit," I growl. "I sure hope you don't feel the way I do."

She laughs. "You'll be happy to know that I don't."

"How bad is it?" I ask.

She adjusts the flow on my IV and shoots me an understanding smirk. "You don't have any skull fractures or intracranial hemorrhage if that's what you're asking—so that's good. You have a really bad concussion and major bruising, but you'll recover."

I fall back against the pillows and wince when I feel more bruising on my ribs and back, but I can feel that I don't have any broken bones there, either, thank Heaven.

She finishes messing around with the equipment. "You have some visitors," she informs me.

"Who is it—the Police? Please tell me those three assholes are in custody."

"They are," she tells me. "Security camera footage from the parking lot caught the whole attack. Police Chief Jim Walker and Detective Eli Hill will be around today or tomorrow to take your statement, but they already said they don't need your testimony to prosecute the three assailants."

I sigh and shut my eyes. "That's good. I wouldn't want Chris to go through that."

"Are you interested in seeing some visitors?" she asks. "I can tell them you don't feel like it."

"Who is it?" I ask. "I don't know anyone in this town."

"It's Fire Chief Brewer and a bunch of people from the Fire Department. They've been waiting for you to wake up."

I brighten up when I think Chris will be with them. "Okay. I guess I can see them."

She leaves and I shut my eyes while I wait. I want to see Chris. I want to make sure she's okay....and I also want to find out how she feels about making out with me in the parking lot.

God, she was so sweet! I can still feel her body rocking against me. I could definitely get used to that.

I'm just drifting into a beautiful fantasy when the door opens. I open my eyes as Chief Brewer, Keith, Danny, Leila, Emily, Caleb, and a dozen other people from the firehouse file into my room.

I keep checking one face after another, but Chris isn't with them. Billy shuts the door last and my heart sinks when they all line up around my bed. She didn't come. Why not?

Chief Brewer grips my shoulder. "Hey, champ. You saved the day again."

I look away. "Naw."

"You're a hero, Josh," Leila tells me. "Admit it."

"I didn't do anything anyone else wouldn't have done," I mumble. "Now I'm laid up in here and I can't do my job."

"You did your job, pal," Chief Brewer replies. "Take all the time you need. We're all grateful to you for saving Chris."

I don't answer. I absolutely refuse to ask him why she didn't come.

"So when are you gonna bring the Batmobile around to the firehouse and let us take it for a spin?" Danny asks and the others laugh.

I bite back a grin, but I don't feel like it. "I can't let you do that, man," I tell him. "I can't let the civilians find out my secret identity."

"At least let us mount the Bat-signal on top of the firehouse," Caleb chimes in. "That would be cool as hell."

I have to laugh. "All right, man. I guess I can do that."

He pumps his fist. "Yes! Do you hear that, John? We're going to send out the Bat-signal instead of having a fire alarm."

"That won't work," Keith interjects. "We'll all already be inside the firehouse. We wouldn't see the signal."

"But Josh will see the signal from Wayne Manor," Ellis points out. "He'll know to mount up in his mask and cape to roll out and conquer evildoers when we give the signal."

Chief Brewer rolls his eyes at me. "You see how it is?"

I find myself chuckling. "Let them have their fun at my expense."

"Expense! Are you kidding me?" Danny counters. "The firehouse couldn't operate without a steady supply of cheesy jokes. We would have to hire you just for that."

"He's already hired," Leila points out.

"That's my point," Danny replies. "Besides, he's such a good sport about it." He turns to me. "Not everyone can hack the endless snark."

"Really?" I ask. "That's the best part."

"We had four different people quit because they couldn't take it," Keith tells me.

"They're idiots," I reply.

"So.....you're cool with everyone calling you the Dark Knight and everything?" Leila asks.

"Is that what they're calling me?"

"They weren't before, but they are now," Chief Brewer replies. "It's either that or the Caped Crusader, the Masked Avenger....."

"The International Man of Mystery....." Keith adds.

I laugh again. "I don't care what you call me as long as no one finds out my secret identity."

"Deal." Chief Brewer squeezes my shoulder again. "Take it easy and heal up. Call me when you're ready to get back to work." He waves to everyone. "Let's leave this man in peace so he can sleep."

He heads for the door and Keith comes forward. He presses my hand once. "Thanks for helping Chris, man. I really appreciate it."

He leaves and Leila bends over to kiss me on the cheek. "You're a hero, Josh. We're all delighted to have you on the crew."

Danny comes over next and clamps me on the shoulder, too. "Take care of yourself, man. We're all pulling for you."

The rest of the crew files past my bed. They congratulate me, thank me for saving Chris, and tell me how much they admire what I did.

My stomach plummets as the last of them finish talking to me and then leave the room. Their sentiments mean a lot after the way I started work at the firehouse. I couldn't ask for a better reception.

None of it means anything, though, because Chris isn't here. I want to see her. I want to hear her thank me for saving her. I want to know she's all right. If she doesn't appreciate what I did, then I don't care what anyone else thinks.

The crew shuts the door and silence falls over the room. I shut my eyes. The pain in my head nags me worse than ever now. The crew's visit tires me out and makes it harder for me to ignore the endless throb.

The letdown of not seeing Chris makes it hurt worse. My spirits crash. This is the last blow.

Maybe I shouldn't have helped her if she doesn't even appreciate it enough to thank me. She doesn't care enough to come and see me in the hospital. She must have just been fooling around with me in the parking lot.

I should have expected that. I shouldn't have gotten my hopes up about her. I should have been more careful when I'm already on the rebound from my last relationship.

I turn my face away, but there's nothing to turn it away from. I'm alone. This is the first time I've been alone for this long in years. I had the life of my dreams not too long ago. Now it's all gone.

I really wish I could fall asleep, but the pain in my head won't let me.

I'm just considering pushing the nurses' call button to tell them to give me some painkillers when the door opens.

I freeze when Chris comes in alone. She has a fat lip and a black eye, but I'm sure she doesn't look as bad as I do.

She comes over to my bed, but she doesn't smile. She looks devastated. "Hi," she chokes and her lips start quivering.

"Hi," I murmur. "Are you okay?"

She nods down at the floor. "I just...." A tear streaks down her cheek.

I try to pry myself off the pillows and end up wincing from the pain in my midsection. "Hey! What's wrong? The crew was just in here. I thought you would be with them."

"I couldn't....I couldn't see you with them around...."

More tears run down her face. I don't know why she's crying.

I force myself to sit up, grab her hand, and pull her toward the bed. "Hey! What's going on?"

She sits down on the mattress next to me. "I.....I had to see you......and tell you......how grateful I am for what you did......I couldn't tell you how I feel in front of them....."

I fall back on the pillows. Oh. It's that. It's just gratitude. She doesn't feel that way about me.

I let go of her hand. "I don't care about anything as long as you're okay. I couldn't let anyone hurt you."

I raise my hand. I want to comb her hair out of her eyes, but I stop myself in time. I can't go there with her—not like that—not if she doesn't feel anything serious about me.

She doesn't mention making out with me in the parking lot, so I don't mention it, either. I guess it was nothing.

She finally rubs her face across the shoulder of her shirt and looks up at me. "I shouldn't keep breaking down around you. How are you? Are you okay?"

"I will be. I feel like crap now, but it will pass and I'll get back on the horse."

"The nurses said you didn't have any broken bones in your face or head."

I nod at nothing. "That's what they said."

She studies me. Her eyes smolder with some emotion I can't identify. She almost looks angry, but I know it's something else.

She waits for me to say something. When I don't, she looks away. "I guess I better go. I just wanted to......thank you....."

"It was nothing," I tell her. "Don't mention it. I would have done the same for anyone."

She nods and looks away. "Thanks. I guess I'll see you back at work."

I murmur, "Yeah."

She mutters, "Bye," and leaves.

I sink back into the pillows and shut my eyes one more time. It sure would have been nice to take it further with her, but I don't want to do that if it's just a meaningless game to her.

I don't fall into the same glum depression, now that she's gone. I harden myself against everything that's happened.

I would have done the same thing for anyone. If I saw some random girl getting attacked in a parking lot, I would have gone after the guys who did it. I would have put them and myself in the hospital to save her. I didn't do anything special because it was Chris.

I don't regret making out with her, either. Now I know it was just casual for her. I can put her out of my mind and stop thinking about her. I can stop wondering if anything could ever happen between us because it never will.

Chapter 8: Chris

I gulp when I read the crew roster on the firehouse noticeboard. I'm scheduled on the rescue truck and the name rostered next to mine pours ice water into my veins. Josh Abbott.

Josh has been in the hospital for a week and at home recovering for three days. Today will be the first day he's come back to work.

I couldn't just ease back into working with him by getting rostered on a different shift. I had to get scheduled to partner with him of all people. This should be one for the record books.

Just then, Brooke comes up to me. "Have you seen the checklist for the drug stores? We're running low on epi and vasopressin."

I tear my gaze away from the roster. "I haven't seen it. Why? Is something wrong with the stores?"

"Someone cleaned out the supplies and now we don't have enough to restock the drug box."

I frown at her. "That's weird. I restocked the drug box the other day after a call. John should have replaced the ampules I took."

"Nope," she tells me. "Could you check it out? I'm worried about going out on a call without them."

We go through every vehicle in the firehouse and check the drug boxes for the rescue truck, the ladder truck, and the two ambulances.

"The drug boxes are okay for the next call," I tell her when we finish. "Let's check the drug cabinet and see what's in there."

I pull my head out of the ladder truck and I'm just about to turn away when Josh walks into the garage. I freeze trying to figure out how to deal with him.

His face is still badly bruised and swollen, but he looks so much better than he did in the hospital.

John walks in at the same time coming from the locker room. "Hey, man!" he greets Josh. "Welcome back!"

They shake hands. "Thanks," Josh murmurs. "It's good to be back."

"If you need to knock off early, you tell me," John goes on. "You can take all the time you need to get back on the horse."

"I'm ready now," Josh replies. "I don't want to sit around on my ass any longer. I'm climbing the walls at home."

John laughs. "I hear you." He claps Josh on the shoulder. "All right. Get to it. Let me know if you need anything."

John walks out of the garage and Josh heads for the locker room. Brooke nudges me. "Aren't you going to ask him about the drugs?"

"Huh?" I turn around. "Why would Josh know about the drugs?"

"John!" she exclaims. "Ask John about the drug order."

"Oh, right!" I race after John and ask him about the drug supplies. He tells me that the stuff is coming in later this week and we can resupply from the hospital if we need to.

I go back inside, but instead of waiting for me to come back with my answer, Brooke is now standing around in a circle with the rest of the crew talking to Josh.

Ellis pretends to hold up his hands in front of his face. "Don't kill me, Batman! I'll change my ways! I swear it!"

Josh laughs. "Cut it out! I'm not Batman."

"Hey!" Danny exclaims. "You said you would bring the Batmobile around for us to test drive."

"No, I specifically said I *wouldn't* bring the Batmobile around for you to test drive," Josh counters. "Don't lie to get in my good books."

"Damn it!" Danny snaps his fingers and grimaces. "Busted again."

They all laugh. I can't go over there, so I pretend to mess around with the truck again. I shouldn't have made out with Josh. Now work is super awkward. Things were going so well between us before, too.

"You and Chris are together on the rescue truck today, man," Caleb tells him.

"I know. I read the roster," Josh replies.

"Just don't go slaying any patients who look at her wrong," Billy chimes in.

Josh changes his tone in a heartbeat. "No one better mess with her while I'm around," he snaps. "If they do, they'll get the same thing."

The atmosphere in the garage changes instantly and a hush falls over the crew.

"Sorry, man," Billy mutters. "I didn't mean it like that."

Josh claps him on the shoulder. "I know."

He walks off and goes to the training room to do something. I pretend not to hear. Did he mean it like that? Did Josh protect me at the pool hall because he feels that way about me—or for something else?

He glossed over our make-out session when I visited him at the hospital. He gave me the impression he wanted to forget it and pretend it never happened—and maybe we should. Maybe it's better that way.

He sure can kiss, though. I have to fight myself not to think about it or I'll wind up getting excited again.

I push those thoughts out of my head when he comes back over to me. "Are you ready to do our start-of-shift checks?" he asks.

"I already did it." I find myself grinning at him. "But you can do it again if you really want to."

"That's okay. I trust you." He climbs into the backseat and rummages around in the bundles of turnouts under the seat.

I fidget trying to decide what to say to him. I really want to walk away, but at the same time, I want to talk to him the way we did before. I want us to get back to the easy way we were getting along before all this happened.

I stick my head back inside the truck. "Hey! We're having another barbecue this weekend. Are you coming?"

He looks up and grins. "You bet. I wouldn't miss it."

That grin makes my heart flip. "Cool!"

He opens the drug box and frowns. "We're short on epi."

"I know. The order hasn't come in yet, but we have enough to keep us going until it comes. We can resupply from the hospital if we need to." Now it's my turn to frown. "You said you weren't going to do a truck check."

He grins even more broadly. "It's habit."

"Why don't you come upstairs to the breakroom and hang out for a while? We haven't seen you in almost two weeks."

His cheeks color and he dips his eyelashes. I didn't mean for that to sound like a suggestion, but I guess I did make it sound like I really missed him—which I did.

He locks the drug box and puts it away, but when he slides across the seat to get out of the truck, the alarm goes off.

"It looks like you're coming to my place after all!" he yells over the noise.

I laugh and climb into the seat next to him. We both start putting on our turnouts as the rest of the crew comes racing downstairs.

"Maybe we'll get a call for a guy with his head stuck through the gap in the steering wheel!" he yells as Keith steers the truck out of the garage.

"Just hope and pray it isn't a guy with his wiener stuck in a beer bottle!" Danny yells over the seat.

We all laugh, but then Billy starts reading the information coming through from dispatch.

"We got a chemical spill main at the Eclipse factory on the west side!" he tells us. "More than four hundred employees have evacuated the building with another hundred trapped inside."

"Get on the horn to the State Emergency Management Bureau!" Keith tells him. "We're gonna need a lot more people!"

He heads out onto the highway, but the Police stop us from going near the factory.

Keith parks there and we suit up in our protective gear. Then we have to walk the rest of the way to the factory parking lot where all the evacuated employees are sitting and lying around on the bare pavement.

"Are there any serious cases that made it out?" Keith asks one of the managers who's helping a woman breathe through her asthma inhaler.

"Those people over there are the ones who inhaled the fumes." The manager points to a dozen people lying under the trees.

Keith waves Naomi and Sophie toward them. "Go check out those people and start transporting them to the hospital. We're going in to get out the trapped patients." He waves at me and Josh. "Come on, you two."

He checks with the manager to find out where the trapped employees are. Josh and I follow Keith to the factory entrance and we go inside with Caleb, Billy, and Danny.

It doesn't take us long to find the patients. They all lie on the floor with froth coming out of their mouths.

Josh and I split up and start checking everyone. The first woman I come to has no pulse and she isn't breathing. I check two more men who are also already gone.

I check ten more people and glance across the room at Josh. He looks up at me behind his protective mask and shakes his head. Damn. We're too late.

We work our way from patient to patient, but they're all dead.

Josh goes over to Keith to give him the news, but from the way the guys are standing on one side of the room not doing anything, it looks like they already know.

I get out the defibrillator and take EKG readings on all the patients just to make sure. They're all flatline. There's nothing we can do here.

Josh waits with the others until I finish and we go outside. We retreat to a safe distance and take off our suits. "That sucks," Keith growls.

"It looks like they died pretty quickly," Josh remarks. "At least they didn't suffer."

"Let's go help transport the other patients," I tell them. "We have to triage all those employees and make sure we didn't miss anyone who might be more critical."

We troop back to the parking lot and give the news to the Police and a few company executives who want to know why we didn't bring out the other employees.

"You'll need to secure the building and make sure it's safe for the Medical Examiner to remove the bodies," Keith tells them.

"Why can't you do that?" the company CEO asks. "Isn't that what you're here for?"

"We treat the sick and injured," Keith growls back. "We don't handle the dead. Besides, we have all these people to take care of." He waves to us. "Come on."

We spend the rest of our shift checking, treating, and transporting more than eighty patients to the hospital. The rest of the employees are healthy enough to leave on their own.

It's already late at night by the time our crew makes it back to the firehouse. We do our best to restock the trucks and ambulances before we get our gear out of our lockers.

Josh comes over to me on our way out of the building. "Are you okay? That was a tough call."

"I'm okay. They were already gone. It's the ones I can't help that get under my skin." I study him. "Are *you* okay? That was a long shift. Are you feeling all right?"

"I'm fine." He looks away. "I'm like you. It's people dying in my hands I can't stand."

I find myself touching his shoulder. "I'm glad you're back. I like working with you. It's really good to know I can count on the other person to hold up their end."

He smiles. "Thanks. I feel the same way about you."

I smile back. "Well, good night. I guess I'll see you tomorrow."

I head out to the parking lot. I'm getting in my car when he comes out of the building.

He walks over to a red pickup truck parked in a corner of the lot. A single streetlamp illuminates the parking lot. He puts his duffel bag in the truck bed and gets out his keys.

Seeing him like this brings back memories of him when we were in the pool hall parking lot. I should have said something about it at the hospital.

I walk over to him. "Josh....."

He turns around and raises his eyebrows at me. "Yeah?"

"I just want to say....I had a really good time with you at the pool hall—and afterward....I mean, before everything went sideways. You know.....when it was just the two of us...."

He stares at me. I can't read his reaction. Does he have any reaction at all? Does he care at all that we made out in the parking lot?

I should just walk away, but the way he's looking at me makes my pulse start racing. I take a chance and lean in and kiss him.

He kisses me back, and before I know what's happening, he threads his fingers into my hair and pulls me in to kiss me harder.

I slip my arms around his waist and press my body against his. I'm still wearing my uniform, but I want to feel him the way did that night. I want to feel that he wants me as much as I want him.

A surge of heat rushes to his crotch the way it did then, but just as fast, he pulls away.

He freezes staring down at me, but his fingers still tangled in my hair hold me away from him now. He doesn't pull me back into his kiss.

"What's wrong?" I choke. I don't want to know.

He lets go of my head and takes a step back. I have no choice but to take my arms away from him. I don't want to. The world goes cold when I feel him moving away from me.

"I'm.....sorry....." I stammer. "I shouldn't have done that."

"Listen. I don't know what it is you want or what you think I want....."

"Nothing!" I blurt out. "I don't want anything!"

"That's the problem, see?"

"No! I don't see! I didn't mean to...." I break off. How did this all go so wrong?

His shoulders sink. "Just listen to me for a second, will you? I thought I was going to marry the girl of my dreams and then the whole thing blew up in my face. I still want that—not with her, but I didn't stop wanting it when she left me. I thought I was going to be a husband and a father and have a house and kids in school and a mortgage and afterschool soccer practice and all of that. Then she pulled the rug out from under me and now I have nothing."

I open my mouth to argue, but he chops his hand to cut me off.

"I still want that," he tells me. "I don't want something casual. I don't know why you kissed me, but if you don't want that—if you don't want to go all in—then just leave me alone, okay? I'm better off alone if I don't have that."

I open my mouth a second time, but the words stop in my throat. I have to think before I fully register what he's saying.

He waits for me to answer and then goes on in a low undertone. "I shouldn't have kissed you at the pool hall. I shouldn't have let it go as far as it did without telling you."

"No! I wanted you to," I blurt out and then break off when I realize what *I'm* saying.

"So....anyway.....now you know," he finishes. "I don't want anything casual. If it isn't serious, I'm not interested."

I nod and shake my hair out of my eyes. "I can respect that."

He waits a minute and then pulls his keys back out of his jacket pocket. "Well, good night. I'll see you tomorrow."

He gets in his truck and starts the motor. I back away as he reverses out of his parking space and drives off into the night.

Chapter 9: Josh

I park my truck in the parking lot at the beach. I'm just getting out when I see Ellen pull up in her car. "Do you want me to carry your cooler down for you?" I ask her.

Her daughter Oakleigh leans over the seat and calls to me through the open window. "Hi, Josh!"

"Hi, munchkin." I turn back to Ellen. "Well? Do you need a man?"

She laughs. "I need a man real bad." She blushes. "Don't tell John I said that."

I grin. "I am so gonna tell him. Pop your trunk."

"Now you're asking for trouble." She pops the trunk and I lift out her cooler.

I carry it down to the beach. A bunch of people are already down there kicking back and shooting the bull like they usually do.

I go over to them and see right away that Chris isn't with them again. Danny hands me a bottle of juice. "Don't worry," he tells me. "I didn't lace it with Kryptonite."

"You saved that for yourself, right?" I tell him. "I hear you have enough decorations to sink the Titanic."

Danny turns bright red. "We don't talk about that."

I'm just about to tease him some more when I hear familiar laughter. I glance across the beach and see Chris talking to some other guy.

He's five inches taller than she is with light brown hair shaved high and tight. He's a big guy totally jacked with muscle and he's wearing a suit—at the beach.

She falls over herself laughing and he snickers at her reaction. They're both drinking beer and he holds a hot dog in one hand.

I get so distracted by watching them that I don't hear what anyone else is saying. The guy says something else and she explodes in screaming laughter. She lunges for him, throws her arms around his neck, hugs him, and kisses him on the cheek.

Seeing them together shouldn't bother me. Nothing is going on between me and Chris. We made out twice. That's it and I'm the one who broke it off last time.

I have no reason to get jealous of her paying attention to some other guy, but watching them makes my blood boil.

I told her how I feel about not wanting anything casual. She said she can respect that—which is a nice way of saying she doesn't want anything serious.

She doesn't have to spell it out for me, but she sure looks serious about that guy. She must be serious about him if she brought him to the firehouse barbecue.

If she's that serious about him, she either led me on behind that guy's back or she moved on him within days of telling me she respects my decision.

I'm not thinking clearly enough to be around people right now. I walk off toward the parking lot and sit in my truck to cool down.

Once I get into it, though, my agitation gets the best of me. I start the engine and drive off without explaining myself to anyone. I drive around town for four hours stewing about her.

I shouldn't care what she does. She's nothing to me. I've been in town less than three weeks and I know nothing about her—except that she isn't serious about me. I don't need to know anything else.

I make up my mind to put her completely out of my mind, but it doesn't work out that way. I spend the whole time fuming about her hooking up with someone else while she was still pretending to be interested in me. I dodged a bullet with that one.

I head back to the firehouse at three o'clock in the afternoon. I'm on the afternoon shift again. At least I won't have to see Chris.

I'm rostered with Leila today. That should be nice and casual. I won't have to worry about any hidden subtext with her.

I put my stuff in my locker and go out to the garage to check the truck. I stop in my tracks when Chris walks in wearing her uniform.

She grins at me like we're best friends or something. "Hi!" she chirps.

"What are you doing here?" I counter. "You aren't rostered today."

"Leila started having cramps. Keith took her to the doctor to get it checked out. I'm covering for her." She frowns at me. "What happened to you? Why did you leave the barbecue?"

I shrug that away. "I just felt like it."

I walk off to the truck, get into the front seat, and start doing the check. She goes to the locker room and then spends ten minutes laughing with her friends. She lets me do the whole check alone. Then she goes up to the breakroom.

She doesn't come downstairs for another full twenty minutes. She sticks her head through the door. "I just got off the phone with John. The drug order still hasn't come in, so he says for us to take the ambulance over to the hospital and steal a bunch of drugs from them. Let's go."

I don't look at her. "Whatever," I reply over my shoulder.

She waits. "Are you coming or what?"

"Okay." I get out of the truck, put the clipboard away, and we get into the ambulance. Sophie and Andy are rostered on the ambulance, so we switch with them.

I sit in the passenger seat and stare out at the road while Chris drives. She doesn't say anything for a minute before she blurts out, "Is something wrong?"

"Nope," I lie. "Everything's great."

She doesn't speak for the rest of the trip. We get our drugs from the hospital and drive back to the firehouse in silence.

I shouldn't be doing this. I can't let resentment get in the way of a work relationship. I have to find some way to put this behind me, but I can't do that when it's all so new and fresh.

She distributes the drugs to the other vehicle drug boxes and locks up the rest in the firehouse drug stores.

I hear her laughing and bantering with the rest of the crew, but I don't join in. I keep out of their way and do busy work.

We go on a few calls and I keep all our interactions strictly professional. I don't joke around with her and she doesn't try to thaw the ice.

If I can just keep this up for a few more weeks and months, this will all blow over. Then neither of us will even remember that we ever did make out.

We finish our shift. Chris is upstairs again when I get my stuff out of my locker and head out to my truck. I put my duffel bag in the back and I'm getting out my keys when she storms out of the building and barges right up to me.

"What the hell is your problem?" she demands.

"What do you mean?" I ask.

"You know exactly what I mean!" she fires back. "You've been giving me the cold shoulder all shift—and don't give me that shit about nothing bothering you. We were fine before the barbecue and then you left without saying anything to anyone. Now you won't talk to me or even look at me."

I start to say, "I don't know what you're talking about. We're talking right now...."

She waves that away. "Don't lie about it, Josh! If you have a problem with me, just spit it out."

"Why would I have a problem? I told you where I stand and you made your choice. I have no reason to resent you for it."

"Resent me!" she counters. "Resent me for what?"

"Look, it's not that big a deal. I told you I don't want anything casual and you said you didn't want anything serious....."

"I never said that!" she exclaims. "I said I respected your decision."

"What's the difference? You got yourself the guy you wanted."

Her jaw drops. "Guy! What guy?"

"I saw you at the barbecue. You don't want to get serious with me and now you got the guy you can be as casual as you want with. I'm happy for you. Have a nice life."

I flip out my truck key and turn back to unlock the door. She stands there with her mouth open watching me put the key in the slot.

"He's my brother!" she blurts out.

I freeze with my hand on the door latch. Shit!

"He's visiting me from out of town. He's come to firehouse barbecues before. That's why he was there. He knows the Brewers and a few other people. He isn't....." She trails off.

My stomach plummets into my shoes. I can't even turn around to face her. Now I know who's the asshole in this and it isn't her.

Her voice trembles so badly that it hurts to listen to her. "I.....I had a fiancé.....before.....He dumped me and left me just like yours did....except that he didn't have any death to explain it away. He just.....left.....and then a week later he got himself engaged to someone else. I don't know if I can......I don't know if I can go through that again."

I spin around before I think to stop myself. "It wouldn't happen again."

"I know.....I just...." She flaps her hands and her eyes swivel around the parking lot without seeing anything. "I can't think of anyone I would rather trust than you. I just.....I got scared, okay? You said you don't want anything casual....and I respect that.....I just don't think I'm there yet."

"Will you ever be?" I ask. "How long has it been? How long do you plan to wait before you try again?"

She opens her mouth to answer, but no sound comes out. Her eyes won't stay on me for more than a few seconds and I realize. She really is scared. She's more than scared. She's petrified.

My heart sinks all over again when I make that connection. She's right. She isn't there yet, and if she isn't there yet, she isn't the right one.

My shoulders relax. "All right," I murmur. "I understand."

She flounders trying to say something or do something—or anything. She's completely lost.

I can't stand seeing her like that. I probably shouldn't, but I walk up to her and put my arms around her. I don't take it any further. I just hold her and feel her trembling in my arms.

She's beautiful—inside and outside. I shouldn't have assumed and I definitely shouldn't have resented her. I should have just accepted wherever she is and whatever she needs to do.

She puts her arms around my waist and buries her face in my jacket. I hear her taking long, shuddering breaths to steady herself.

I want to help her somehow. I want to help her get through this.

For no reason, I kiss her on the head. I care about her. That's the truth. I just want her to be happy and safe even if she doesn't wind up with me. I have to remember that.

She finally straightens up and I let her go. She uses one finger to push her hair out of her face. It falls back into place in a perfect curve around her cheek and jawline. She's by far the most beautiful woman I've ever met in a down-to-earth, practical way.

Some power greater than myself steers me close to her and I kiss her. She stiffens and then melts. I don't know why I'm doing this, but it feels right.

I don't maul her and devour her the way I did before. I don't know why, but it feels different this time.

She goes into it much more slowly, but the heat and emotion spikes much more quickly than last time if that's even possible. I pull her against me and she puts her arms around my neck the way she did before.

She's wearing her uniform, so touching her doesn't feel the same. She felt so exquisite in that short skirt. Now her uniform gets in my way, but that only makes me so much more aware of the beautiful soul hidden underneath.

I don't understand the way I feel about her, but I want her. I want a lot more than just making out in parking lots. I have to stop doing that with her.

As soon as I pull her against me, the energy and tension hidden under her clothes erupts. She tries to hold it back, but I feel it anyway.

I spin her around and pin her against the truck. I want to take her, but not like this. I don't want it ever to be like this between us.

She stiffens when I get her into that position, and when I push into her, she breaks away from my mouth. Her features contort. "Don't!"

I back off immediately. "Sorry," I murmur. "I thought you wanted to."

"It's just....Patrick did that....."

My scalp prickles at the name....and then I remember. He was doing that to her when I found him. He pinned her against his car like that. He would have kidnapped her if I hadn't intervened.

"I'm really sorry," I tell her. "I should have remembered."

"I do want to, but I don't want to step on your toes. I don't want you to do something you're going to regret later."

"I won't regret it," I tell her and I've never been more certain of anything. "You're special to me."

She looks up at me with huge eyes. "You're special to me, too."

"I want you," I tell her. "I want you real bad. I feel....something for you."

"Are you sure?" she asks. "Are you sure you want to do this?"

I nod. "I'm sure."

She gulps again. I have to have her. This is right. I don't know why, but I feel that.

I lean in and kiss her again. She responds, but the emotion in that kiss is like nothing I've ever felt. It goes so far beyond what we did at the pool hall.

I want to grab her and touch her and grope her again, but I can't do it here—not right outside the firehouse.

This time, I'm the one who pulls away. "Get in my truck," I tell her.

She turns away immediately, walks around to the passenger side, and gets in while I slide behind the wheel and start the motor.

Chapter 10: Chris

I can't look at Josh when he parks his truck at the beach. The fire crew just had their latest barbecue here earlier today, but Josh only came for a few minutes before he left.

He thought my brother was....more than that. Josh got jealous. He really does want something from me.

I don't have to wonder what he wants because he told me. Am I ready for that?

I know I'm not ready for it, but it looks like we're doing this whether we're serious or not.

I can't stop thinking about what he said—and about what I said. He said I'm special to him and I told him the same thing.

He *is* special to me. I trust him. I respect him. I'm attracted to him. I don't know what that means, but he's special to me and I don't want to lose him—whatever that means.

Now we're here at the beach in the middle of the night. He gets out of the cab and I get out on my side. The dome light switches off and darkness falls over the beach.

The surf booms in the darkness and I hug my arms around my body to block out the chill. I'm still wearing my uniform and jacket, but I can't stop shaking.

I'm here with Josh and I don't know what's going to happen next. One thing I know for sure. I trust him. I like him—a lot. I want to find out what happens next. I want whatever happens next—whatever it is

.

He comes over to me, takes my hand, and leads me out onto the beach. The light from town shines off the clouds and gives just enough of a glow for us to see where we're going. I can see him in the gloom, too.

We walk along the sand going nowhere in particular. We're just here together and that's saying a lot. It's a lot better than it was earlier today when he wouldn't even look at me.

"I'm sorry I assumed about your brother," he murmurs after a while. "I'm a jerk."

"It's okay," I reply. "I was really worried when you stopped talking to me. I don't want that to happen between us again. I thought I did something to offend you."

"You did—in my mind. I thought you were either playing me or that you hooked up with someone else right after you were kissing me. I was pissed."

I squeeze his hand. "I wouldn't do that. Shit, I haven't been able to look at a guy since my fiancé left."

"Do you think he had the other woman standing by waiting?"

I shrug. "I guess it doesn't really matter, does it? If he didn't and he just shacked up with her a week after dumping me, then that's just as bad as if he did have her standing by waiting, isn't it?"

He looks out over the surf. "Sometimes I wonder if my fiancé had someone else."

"Why would she? You said she was happy right up until her brother died."

"That's what I thought. Then, at other times, I wonder if maybe she had someone else and she just used her brother's death to dump me. I mean, she was going to marry me. She made me think she never wanted anything or anyone else. Then she walked out on me when I needed her most. If she really was that devastated over her brother's death, why not turn to me? I was the one person who understood what she was going through. I was the one person she could rely on. Why walk out on that?"

"I know," I murmur. "It makes no sense."

He looks away again. "I shouldn't be talking about her when I'm here with you."

"I don't mind. I'm talking about my ex. You might as well."

He turns around and gazes down at me. "Thanks for being so understanding. I wouldn't blame you if you pushed me away from being such a jerk."

"You weren't being a jerk. You did it because you care."

He eases close to me. "Yeah. I do."

He passes his fingertips down my hair and then lets them drag over my lips. His eyes glide down to my mouth, but he doesn't kiss me.

I wait while he stands there studying me. Then he turns aside and starts walking again.

Walking down the beach holding hands in the dark feels so intimate. It feels so much more intimate even than hooking up in a parking lot.

Is this all he wants to do? I don't want to push him. I don't even really want to do it with him. This feels so much better—so much closer even than doing it with him.

This is the first time we've been close like this—closer than physical. I don't want it to end. I don't want to spoil it even by kissing him.

This feels so touching and achingly sweet—just us being here and both of us knowing we care about each other. We care about each other in that way. Knowing it means a lot.

After a while, he turns away from the waves, hikes up the beach, and sits down on the dry sand. He pulls me down next to him and puts his arms around me, but he doesn't do anything else. He doesn't even kiss m e.

We sit in silence listening to the waves pound. I don't expect him to say anything else. I don't need him to say anything else. This is enough—this right here.

He startles me out of my thoughts. "Can I tell you something?"

"Sure—anything."

"I've never told anyone....."

I tense. What is he going to tell me?

"I think I was more broken up over losing him than I was over losing her. Isn't that terrible? I cared more about losing him than I did about losing her. I would much rather have him back than her."

"I don't think it's terrible at all. He was your best friend and your work partner for years."

"The weird thing is that I could have talked to him about losing her. If she just left and broke my heart, I could have talked to him and he would have understood. He would have told me it wasn't me, but I didn't have that."

I put my arms around him. "Maybe the way he died had something to do with it."

He looks away. "Maybe. I never talked to her about my calls. I always talked to him about it because he was there and understood ....and I never talked to her about *that* call. I never talked to her about what happened in the building. The rest of our crew had to drag me out of the building kicking and screaming to stop me from going back in there to get him even though it was too dangerous. The whole house went up. I would have been burned to a crisp if they didn't take me out when they did.....and we never recovered his body. He got completely vaporized in there after they took me out."

I sit listening in silence. Damn. That must have been hard—to work your ass off trying to save your best friend, only to have them snatched from in front of your eyes. I can only imagine how hard that must have been.

"I could have talked to him about that in ways I couldn't talk to her. I had to protect her from finding out exactly what happened to him. She never found out that I tried to save him or that I would rather have stayed in a burning building with him than save my own life. I could never tell her that."

I squeeze him again. "I'm glad you can tell me. I would never want you to keep something like that from me."

He looks down at me. His eyes look ghostly in this darkness. Now I can see how his friend's death haunts him. It isn't so obvious in daylight when he looks like a normal guy.

He kisses me once, stands up, and tugs my hand to pull me to my feet. Then he sets off down the beach.

"I've never gotten involved with another paramedic before," he remarks after a while.

"Neither have I," I admit. "My ex wasn't involved in emergency work....and I never talked to him about my calls, either. I never wanted to burden him with all that."

"Maybe it's a curse," he mutters to the waves.

"How can it be a curse if it brings us closer together—all of us? I share that with the people on my crew. It's like you say. I don't have to explain anything to them. It was like that after we lost that burn victim. I didn't have to explain anything to you because you already knew why it bothered me."

"Yeah," he mutters. "I know."

I squeeze his hand again. Now I know why and how he knows about the burn victim. "I'm sorry I couldn't have been there for you that way after that call. Were you okay about seeing those guys burned?"

"Yeah, I was fine. I never had to see my friend afterward, thank God. I probably would have had to quit the fire service if I had."

I look away. I don't want to talk about it.

"Sorry," he tells me. "I shouldn't have said that."

I don't want to talk about it, so I don't answer. I'm just wondering how to change the subject when he stops me and turns to face me.

He eases up close to me again, runs his fingertips down the side of my face, and then takes very gentle hold of my jaw to pull my mouth to his lips. He kisses me and that kiss doesn't stop.

We're alone on the beach in the middle of the night. No one will see us here.

He takes his time kissing me. He doesn't hurry and that kiss tells me that he won't break off or pull away this time.

When he does stop kissing me, his eyes burn into my soul. He means it. He isn't fooling around or testing the waters.

He eases back just a little bit, takes hold of my jacket, and starts to pull it off. He slides it off my arms and leaves me standing there in my T-shirt.

He drops my jacket on the ground, lifts my T-shirt over my head, and lets it fall on top of the jacket.

The cold air bites my skin and I shiver. The surf sounds extra loud.

He keeps his eyes locked at me at all times. I can't look away when he holds my gaze like that. He's doing it. He said he wants me. He's going to take me right here on the beach.

He unclips my bra with a flick of his fingers. Then he slides his fingers ever-so gently under my bra straps, eases them off my shoulders, and pulls my bra off.

My nipples harden in the cold. I expect him to touch me, but he doesn't. His gaze ranges down my neck over my chest and stomach. He studies me closely and then drops onto his knees.

He takes off my boots and socks and stays down there to unbutton my pants, slide them down my legs, and then pull them over my feet.

He lays all my clothes in a pile next to me until I'm standing in front of him stark naked in the freezing sea air.

The surf pounds in my ears and my heart hammers. I can barely breathe.

He stands up in front of me extra slowly and his eyes bore into me just as intensely. What does he see when he looks at me? Does he like what he sees? Am I good enough for him?

He raises his hand and trails his fingertips down my cheek again. He kisses me, but only once and he doesn't stay there.

He strokes his flat, warm palm over my shoulders, down my arms, and across my chest. He takes extra long to get as far as my breasts.

He watches me gasp and pant when he brushes his palms very gently against my rock-hard nipples. I gulp down rising excitement. I can hardly stand the way he's looking at me, but I have to stand before him and let him see me react to his touch.

He rotates his palms across my nipples to roll the hard little nubs. He can feel how hard and sensitive they are. Does it turn him on to see how much he excites me? Does he like it when he makes me moan and spasm under his hand?

He brushes the soft backs of his knuckles down my stomach and over the sensitive skin between my legs. I whimper in aching need. I'm already soaking wet.

Before I can react, he slips his left hand into my hair, grips me by the back of the neck, and holds me while his other hand burrows between my legs.

My wetness gushes around his fingers and he starts rotating them fast to drive me to the stars. I moan in ecstasy while he plunges into me and makes me quake and shudder on his hand.

"Look at me, baby," he murmurs. "Look at me and let me see how much you want me."

My eyes drift open, but they keep losing focus as he drills me deeper and harder. I can't stop swooning in his hands.

He controls me by the head and I buck my hips against his hand trying to take him all the way in. I sob and scream out to the waves as he brings me to a crushing climax.

I can't stop screaming as he pumps his fingers all the way in. I'm still moaning and teetering on unsteady legs when he lets go of me.

I struggle to catch my balance, but he doesn't help me. He takes a step back and starts pulling off his jacket.

He throws it on the pile of my clothes followed by his T-shirt. His muscles stand out in the shadowy light while he tugs his belt off.

He kicks his boots into the same pile, steps on his pant cuffs, and steps out of them so he stands in front of me naked.

I don't know what he's going to do. My head still swims from the orgasm he just gave me.

He looks at me for one instant, steps back into position, wraps his warm arms around me, and lifts me off my feet to kiss me.

I succumb to that kiss as never before. Now I can drift in the blissful haze of all this desire sweeping over me.

He kisses me ravenously, hungrily—the way he did at the pool hall. Now there's nothing left to stand between us.

All that desire erupts out of me. I want him so bad and now I know he wants me, too. We're naked together on the beach with no one else around. I can give myself to this and hold nothing back.

He pumps into me and I feel again how hard and strong he is. He doesn't hold back, either. His tongue sizzles in my mouth and I feel that hot wetness translating between my legs.

I ache for him to take me and he complies by pulling my thighs on either side of his waist. His hardness touches me and then he lets me sink onto it.

I scream at the colossal intensity of it and then he's pulling me into his thrusts. He collapses onto his knees with me riding his hips as he pumps upward into me in a steady, unbroken rhythm.

I can't kiss him. I'm screaming too much from every powerful thrust. He seizes my hair by the back of my head, pries my head back, and mauls me down my neck, bites my breasts, and crawls back up to my mouth.

The feeling of my thighs straddling him drives me out of my mind and I lose all control. I can't stop hurling myself against him again and again until I explode all over him.

He keeps driving through it all. I need him to keep going forever and ever and never stop. I can't get enough of this.

He grabs one of my breasts and guides it into his mouth. The sensation spikes me over the edge again. I grab his shoulders and try to control his head, but there's no stopping him.

He seizes my wrist, twists it behind me, and uses that and my hair to guide me where he wants me to go.

The feeling of his fingers in my hair reminds me of Patrick. A rush of terror grips me all over, but then I remember. This isn't Patrick.

It's Josh. I'm safe with him. I trust him. He would never hurt me. He wouldn't do any of this if I didn't want him to.

I collapse into him, and right at that moment—almost as if he read my mind—he lets go of both my wrist and my hair.

I topple forward and my forehead falls on his shoulder. I can't cope with all the sensations rushing through me right now. I feel.....I don't know what I feel for him, but I know one thing.

This isn't casual anymore. Maybe it never was.

I don't know if it's as serious as he says he wants it to be, but I can't think of this as casual.

He rubs the back of my neck, pets my hair, and kisses the side of my head, but he never stops pumping into me. He keeps up that steady rhythm that sends one torrent of overpowering sensation after another rocketing through me.

I whimper in an agony of mind-blowing emotion and pleasure. He can't be doing this to me. He can't be giving me the most beautiful night of my life when we've only just met.

He wraps his arms around me and hugs me against him, but he never stops. His deep, resounding thumps blast me to the stratosphere all over again.

I whine and whimper on his shoulder until the power builds to a catastrophic climax. I howl in his ear, but I can't hold myself up.

He crushes my body in his arms moving me up and down on his strokes. I reel under the sheer power of that assault. I scream myself hoarse. I can't contain it. I have to let it pour out of me in epic surges that never stop.

I buckle in his embrace still howling and almost weeping in rapture. I've never felt this with anyone.

He kisses the side of my head again, and when I can't raise my head to kiss him back, he does it for me.

He closes my head in both hands, pries my head up, and holds me there while he kisses me. He keeps gliding in and out of me endlessly. Does he ever plan to stop? Does he plan to possess me like this and conquer me all night long? I don't know if I can deal with that.

I'm still whimpering and convulsing with overwhelming energy when he closes me in his arms again, rises on his knees, and lays me back on the sand. He crawls up between my legs without pulling out.

He kisses me and his body undulates between my legs while he plows me out of this world all over again.

He tears off my mouth and pushes himself up on his muscular arms. He stares down at me, snatches a kiss from me, and looms over me to stare down at me.

He watches me grimace and scream every time he blasts me to another crescendo of pleasure and earth-shattering ecstasy. Does he even realize how amazing he is?

I claw at his chest trying to cope with everything he's doing to me. I can't stop screaming as I blast over the edge in another tempest of climax.

"Come on, baby!" he orders. "Come on! Let me hear you scream for me!"

I'm already screaming as loud as I can. The louder I scream, the more I shatter in one orgasm after another. I've had so many that I can't stop now.

He keeps calling on me to scream for him and give myself to him. I can't scream or give myself to him any more than I already am, but that's not the point.

He arches down to kiss me and stays locked on my mouth. I swim out of my delirium long enough to hear him groaning as his own energy escalates. He throbs inside me, and with one deep thrust, he drives all the way in.

His hot essence floods me and he roars into my mouth. That feeling of him pulsating and spasming inside me electrifies me even more and I explode in another blistering climax right along with him.

He immediately starts stroking in and out of me again, but more slowly. Now I feel his slippery cocktail mixing with mine. It gushes all over my thighs that are still wrapped around his waist. That wetness seeps into the sand underneath me.

That sensation turns me on as never before. I want more of him. I never want him to stop, but in a second, he rolls off me onto his back.

He pulls me with him so I lie straddling on top of him. I can't move, so I melt on top of him, bury my face in his neck, and let the blissful waves of rapture wash over me.

The heat radiating off his chest keeps me warm even in the cold air. He wraps one arm around my back and his other hand clasps the back of my neck. He presses me into his body.

He's already going soft, but I don't move. I just want to lie here with him and feel this. I don't even know what this is, but I need it. I need it like nothing else I've ever felt.

He lifts his head just long enough to kiss my hair and then flops back on the sand. His heart pounds against my ear. I don't need anything but this. I don't need anything but to feel him near me and holding me like this.

Chapter 11: Josh

I wake up and stare at the grey dawn sky. I don't remember right away where I am....and then I feel Chris lying on top of me. We're both naked and she's still straddling me.

I glance at my watch. It's five-fifteen in the morning. We've been here all night.

That was one of the best night's sleep I've had in a long time. I don't want to leave, but we both have to work today. In fact, we have to work together today.

I kiss the side of her head. My God, she is so damn sweet! I want to hold her like this always. "Wake up, baby. Wake up. We gotta go to work."

She groans and buries her face in my neck. "Don't say that word," she growls.

I laugh. "What about, 'coffee'? Can I say that word?"

She laughs under my ear. "Throw in a triple shot of espresso and I might be interested."

"I know somewhere you can get that—and a shower."

"Do I have to die and go to Heaven first?"

"No, you can come to my place."

Her head snaps up and she stares at me. Her hair is all rumpled, but she looks absolutely gorgeous like this. I want to see her like this every morning.

"Are you fooling with me?" she husks.

"No, I have an espresso machine.....and a shower. You just have to get up and get dressed."

"You must be the devil." She runs her fingers through her hair, climbs off me, and sits down on the sand to pull her clothes on.

I sit up, too, and in a second, we get back in my truck and drive to my house. She follows me inside and looks around my living room. "This is so not what I was expecting."

"What did you expect?"

She saunters into the house looking at the couches in the living room, the heavy slab of cypress wood that makes up the coffee table, the rock garden in the center of the dining room table, and the shiny espresso machine on the kitchen counter.

"I don't know what I expected, but it wasn't this." She goes over to the bookshelf and smiles when she sees pictures of my family. "Aw. This is nice."

"Someone in the world still loves me." I shut the front door. "Go take a shower. I'll make the coffee. The bathroom is down there."

I point to the hall leading to my bedroom. I'd like nothing better than to take her in there, strip her naked, and make her scream like she did last night, but we both have to go to work in an hour.

She leaves and I get started making her a giant cappuccino with extra espresso, extra chocolate syrup, and extra whipped cream. That should get her engines fired up for the day if nothing else does.

The shower switches on down the hall. I drift into a blissful memory of last night on the beach with her. Mmmm. She's perfect.

I have to think about something else so I don't start getting hard for her again. I catch myself thinking about going down the hall, climbing into the shower with her, and bumping her against the tiles until she screams again....and again....and again.

Damn it. Work today is going to get complicated.

She comes out with her hair all wet and her skin glowing. She grins when I put the cappuccino in front of her. "Now I know you're the devil."

I take a gulp of mine. "I gotta take a shower. Make yourself at home until I get back."

I take a shower and come out to find her looking at the pictures on the shelf again. She stands in front of pictures of me and my friend. One of them is a picture of me and him with his sister.

"What was his name?" she asks me.

I look away. "His name was Chris."

She spins around to stare at me, but she doesn't make a sound. I see her out of my peripheral vision. She stands there gaping at me in horror. Now she knows.

I go back to the kitchen and down a few shots of espresso. She shakes herself out of her trance, wanders around the living room drinking her drink, and eventually comes over to wash out her glass in the sink.

She sticks the glass upside down in the dish drain. "It's six-thirty," she tells me. "Are you ready to go?"

"Yeah, I'm ready. Let's get out of here."

I turn to leave, but she sidesteps in front of me to stop me. She looks up at me with eyes overflowing with understanding and sympathy.

This is the final frontier—being around someone with the same name as my dead friend—someone whose presence will constantly remind me of him.

She doesn't say a word. She cups my face in both her hands and kisses me. That kiss tells me so painfully that she understands. She understands what it means.

She lets me go and we both walk out of the house, get in my truck, and drive to the firehouse.

Her car sits in the parking lot exactly where she left it. She waits for me to take my duffel bag out of the truck bed and then we walk inside together.

No one is in the garage yet. We hear the night shift upstairs taking showers, making breakfast, and laughing.

Chris shoots me a grin and goes to get the truck checklist. "Are you ready to act professional?"

"Around you? Never."

She giggles and blushes. "Just don't start making jokes about getting your wiener stuck in a beer bottle."

I burst out laughing and feel my cheeks burning. "Can we not call it that?"

She explodes with laughter just as Danny, Ellis, and Caleb come downstairs. "What's so funny?" Danny asks.

I turn back to the truck. "Nothing."

"It sure looks like something." He looks back and forth between us and his expression changes, but he doesn't say anything.

I climb inside and start doing the checklist. Chris gets down to work, too. We both work on the truck check, but we don't seem to be able to stop laughing for no reason anytime we're within sight of each other.

No one says anything about it, but it sure is looking obvious. I'm just noticing Keith scowling at us when the fire alarm saves us.

We jump in the truck and head out into town. "What do we got?" he yells at Billy.

"Building fire downtown!" Billy hollers back. "Employees trapped inside! Looks like a job for Superman."

"Superman is on vacation!" I yell back. "Call back on Thursday. You might have better luck."

Some of the guys laugh. "Superman doesn't take vacations, pal," Danny tells me.

"Then it's a good thing I'm not him." I pull on my turnouts, stick on my helmet, and glance over at Chris while I buckle it under my chin.

She's ready to roll in her turnouts. Her eyes sparkle under her helmet and she smiles at me while she adjusts her breathing apparatus.

We're going to need them. Keith parks the truck down the block from the scene and we see black smoke billowing from the building in question.

The Police hustle over to us when we get out of the truck. "The fire broke out on the fifteenth floor!" one of the officers yells to us. "We don't know which floors are involved or how far the fire has spread. The employees who were working on the ground floor all got out okay. They say one of the floors collapsed and everyone above that floor is still trapped inside."

"What about the emergency stairwells?" Keith asks.

He shrugs. "I don't know. We haven't sent anyone in. We were waiting for you guys."

Keith waves behind us and calls Brooke and Naomi over. "We'll split up into two teams—one for each emergency stairwell. That way, if one stairwell is still intact, at least one team can get through."

"And if neither stairwell is intact?" Danny asks.

"Then we'll need to find that out so we can decide how to get up there." He squints at the building. "The fire is moving up, not down.

We should be good below that floor. Chris and Josh—you go with Danny, Caleb, Ellis, and Billy. The rest of you come with me."

We split up and enter the lobby. The sprinklers are still blasting water all over the place.

We divide and start climbing the emergency stairwells. Everything goes fine until we get to the fifteenth floor.

"The stairwell is intact here," Danny points out. "That means the fire must be cutting off the employees from getting out."

"How do you want to do this?" Caleb asks.

"We'll just have to search each floor," Danny decides. "Put on your SCBAs."

We all fit our breathing apparatuses over our faces and he pulls the door open. We walk out into an ordinary office level full of cubicles and workspaces.

We search everywhere, but we don't find any trace of the lost employees or the fire. Everything looks normal.

We start working our way up one floor at a time. Searching takes a long time.

We meet back up at the stairs and Danny's radio crackles. "Are you in?" Keith asks.

"We're in!" Danny calls through his radio. "The stairs on this side are intact, but we're searching for the employees and not finding them."

"The stairs are destroyed on this side. We're on our way over to you," Keith replies.

Danny signs off. We head up to the next floor.

It looks normal near the stairs, but when we get to the far side of the floor, we discover half the story caved in.

Danny frowns at it. "We should have seen this from the floor below. Something's wrong. We need to pull out until we secure the building."

"What about the employees?" Ellis asks.

"We'll have to come up with a better way to find them. I don't want us getting trapped in here, too. Get back to the stairs."

We turn around to head back. We cross most of the floor and Danny opens the door leading to the stairwell.

He holds it open and Billy and Ellis pass through to leave the floor. Caleb is just about to pass through when the floor rumbles beneath my feet. I freeze, and at that moment, the floor behind me implodes.

I spin around just as Chris falls through the gap. A massive woof of flames and smoke erupts from underneath. It must have been eating away inside the building's structure between the floor and the ceiling underneath.

She screams and that sound sets off my survival instinct. I take a massive lunge and skid across the floor. "CHRIS!!" I bellow and dive for the crumbling edge of the floor.

I catch her by the wrist before she plummets. Five more floors below have already collapsed.

She spins there screaming at the end of my hand. "HOLD ON!!" I tell her.

"JOSH—HELP ME!!" she shrieks.

"HOLD ON!! I GOT YOU!!" I roar, but I won't be able to hold her forever.

Heat licks my cheeks from a few feet away. Flames billow from the lower floors. They're coming from beyond the cave-in or we'd both be dead already.

The fire must have been inside the walls. We searched every floor below this. We wouldn't have missed this. The building just crumbled right now.

I glance behind me to see Danny and Caleb sprinting toward us, but right at that moment, the ceiling above their heads buckles. Debris and broken frame timbers rain in front of them and cut them off from getting near me and Chris.

I gulp as the truth sets in. I'm on my own here.

Chapter 12: Josh

C hris swivels, looks down, and then flings up her other arm to grab my hand in both of hers. I already feel my strength ebbing. I need to pull her up now before I lose all my strength.

I heave with all my might, roll onto my side, and haul her one painful inch at a time. She sprawls back on the floor next to me panting and whimpering in terror. Then she looks around and sees the building caved in behind us.

"We're trapped," she husks.

"We gotta find a way to get back to the stairwell," I gasp. "Come on."

I try to stand up, but I'm shaking too badly from nerves and exhaustion. I can't lose her—not like this. I can't lose Chris—not again.

She grabs my shoulders and helps me up. We stagger toward the cave-in and search around it for a way to get to the stairs. The stairwell entrance is completely blocked off.

We work our way into the neighboring offices, but none of them connects up with any hallway leading to the stairwell.

We meet back up in the building's main corridor outside the cave-in. "What do you want to do?" Chris asks.

I glance around, but right then, the floor buckles underneath us. I topple sideways.

Lightning quick, Chris dives for me, grabs me by the turnouts, and drags me toward her. I pitch across her and we both land hard on the floor just as the section buckles where I was just standing.

I fall on top of her and she groans in pain. "Are you okay?!" I yell. "Are you hurt?"

She doesn't have time to answer before another blast of fire explodes from the floor beneath us. I scramble to get off her, pull her to her feet, and we both run for it, but the floor is collapsing too fast.

The fire gnaws the building to pieces one inch at a time. We back away into a conference room and I slam the door, but the fire rushes me from outside. It will eat its way into this room any second now.

Chris rushes to the windows. "We have to get out somehow!"

"We can't get out that way," I tell her. "We're almost twenty floors up. We'd be just as dead."

"We're dead either way." She turns to face me and our eyes meet.

I'm glad I'm here with her. I'm glad no one will pull me out of this building while she gets trapped in here alive. That would be my worst nightmare all over again.

I'm just about to open my mouth to tell her how I really feel about her when her eyes swivel upward. "There, Josh!"

"Huh?" I ask. "What do you mean?"

"The ceiling! The cave-in only took out this floor. We can crawl through the ceiling to the next floor up. We can get to the stairwell that way."

I frown at her. "Are you sure?"

"Come on!" She climbs onto the conference table and stretches her arms toward the ceiling tiles. One of them has been replaced with the grate leading to a ventilation duct, but she isn't tall enough to reach it.

She glances around and grabs one of the big chairs standing by the table. "Come on!!" she yells. "Hurry!"

She sets the chair under the ventilation grate, climbs onto the chair, and pushes the grate upward. From here, she can climb into the ventilation duct.

"I sure hope you're right about this," I tell her.

"We have nothing to lose."

I climb up after her and crawl into the duct. We have to lie flat on our stomachs to fit into it. "Don't breathe," she tells me.

I have to laugh. "I'll try not to."

We inch our way along and get to a duct leading upward to the next floor. "Of course they didn't put any ladder in here for us to climb up," she mutters.

"That would be too easy," I tell her.

"Okay, get out your Superman cape and fly us up there," she teases.

I snort. "If I could fly, I would have broken that window and we'd be on the ground right now."

She strips off her breathing apparatus and wriggles out of the harness. "We'll just have to climb up."

I crawl over next to her to see. "It's a long way up."

"Hey, how about you be a gentleman and I'll stand on your head to get to the next level."

I laugh again. "I don't think I'm ready for that kind of commitment yet."

She smirks and me and then her smile evaporates. "Josh?"

"Yeah?" I ask.

"I do want to go all in with you.....I'm just scared."

I grab her and kiss her. I want to tell her so many things, but now isn't the right time.

I ease back and gaze into those magnetic eyes. "Take your time, baby. I'll wait as long as it takes for you to be ready."

She stares at me even harder, and all at once, we both rush each other. I grab her and kiss her with all my might and she does the same thing.

She crushes me hard enough to hurt me, but it feels good. We need each other and not just to get out of this building.

We pull apart and she smiles at me before she sits up. She leaves her SCBA lying there in the duct. She can't climb with it on. She starts wedging herself up the duct to the next floor above.

I take the time to crawl out of my SCBA. I hear her turnouts squeaking on the slippery metal.

I squirm over there to see what she's doing. Her turnouts actually grip the sides and make it easier for her to get a purchase on the duct's sides.

She finally flops into the next horizontal stretch of duct above us. "I'm there!" she pants. "Come on up!"

"Take a look around and see if you can find a way to the stairs," I tell her and start climbing.

Now it's my turn. I brace myself against the duct's sides and discover the same thing. My turnouts stick to the metal. It's the perfect anchor to propel myself higher.

"I found it!" Chris tells me when I collapse panting in the duct next to her. "I found the grate leading down to the stairwell. We can get there."

I crawl over to her and we look down through the grate. It opens into the main corridor right outside the stairwell.

Just then, I hear voices behind me. I pivot around and stare. "Did you hear that?"

We both strain our ears to listen. "It sounds like at least one of them is a woman," Chris whispers. "That must be the employees."

I crawl toward the sound and Chris follows me. We cross most of the floor and look down into a different conference room.

Four women and five men huddle on the floor. A sixth man stands by the window. "The Fire Department is outside," he tells the others. "They're sending people into the building." He crosses the room and sits down with the other employees. "They'll come for us. We just have to hold out a little longer."

"We can save them," Chris whispers. "We have to save them before any more of the building collapses."

"The floor must have collapsed down there," I tell her. "That's the only reason they wouldn't be trying to get to the stairs."

"We can bring them up here," she replies. "We can get them through the duct to the stairwell."

I grin at her and steal one last kiss. "You're brilliant. Let's do it. You go first. They won't be as scared of you."

She laughs and starts lifting out the grate. The employees don't see her until she sticks her head down into the conference room.

"Hey!" she calls out.

They all look up.

"I'm Chris Daniels!" she tells them. "I'm a paramedic with the Howe County Fire Department. My partner and I are here to get you out of the building."

They all jump up exclaiming in relief. One woman bursts into tears. "Oh, thank God!" she whimpers.

"Get one of the chairs and put it on the table underneath this grate," Chris instructs them. "Then you can climb up here. My partner will show you where to go."

They hustle to obey her and one of the women stands on the chair. I crawl back to the grate by the stairwell.

The woman's head comes through and Chris helps her climb into the duct. "Crawl over there to my friend. His name is Josh. He'll help you get to the stairs."

The woman sobs in relief all the way over to me. "Lower your legs through first," I tell her. "I'll hold onto your hands and let you down the rest of the way. Okay?"

She nods fast and does exactly what I tell her. I take hold of both her wrists, lower her to the floor, and point to the stairwell. "Take those stairs to the ground level. You might meet some firefighters coming up from below. Go!"

"Oh, thank you!" she exclaims, but I don't have time to talk to her before the next woman crawls over to me.

My heart starts racing as one person after another comes toward me, drops down, and disappears into the stairwell. We're doing it.

I just dread the moment when the building explodes with me and Chris still inside it—or just Chris inside it. Every passing minute makes it more likely that this rescue will end that way.

Finally, the last man crawls over to me and I lower him down. I look up to find Chris smiling at me. Her whole face glows. "I guess that makes me Superwoman."

I kiss her one more time. "Get out of here. That's an order."

She swings her legs over the side and I take hold of her wrists. I drop her to the floor and she waves me down. "Come on."

I jump down next to her, snatch one more kiss, and we rush into the stairwell. We meet Keith, Danny, Billy, Caleb, and Brooke coming up to meet us.

"Are you two all right?" Keith asks. "Danny said you got trapped up there."

"We did, but we got out," I tell him.

"Did you get all the employees?" Keith asks.

"All the employees we could find," I reply. "The building is too unstable to go back to look for anyone else. We barely made it out."

He claps me on the shoulder. "You're a hero."

"Actually, this one was Chris's. She was the one who found them and got them out."

Chris blushes. "We both did."

"All right. Let's get out of here," Keith orders.

I catch Chris looking at me on our way downstairs. I want to hold her hand, but I can wait on that. I can wait for all of it.

Chapter 13: Chris

I come downstairs from the breakroom and head for the training room to meet up with the rest of the crew. We're doing an inspection of all the SCBAs since our last call-out to the burning building.

I'm just about to go inside when my brother Zack walks up the driveway and enters the garage. "Hey!" I greet him. "What brings you over here?"

"I'm just about to leave town," he tells me. "I just came to say goodbye."

"Aw!" I moan. "Can't you stick around a little longer?"

"Nope. Duty calls."

"To hell with duty. I need you here."

He laughs at me. "That's rich coming from you. No one is more dedicated to duty than you are."

I grin at him, but just then, John's support pickup pulls into the driveway. Josh and Danny get out and start unloading the new oxygen tanks, masks, and regulators John ordered to replace the units Josh and I left in the burning building.

"Hey, Josh!" I call out. "Come here! I want to introduce you. This is my brother, Zack Daniels. Josh is the guy I told you about—from the pool hall parking lot."

Zack sticks out his hand. "It's an honor to meet you. You're a hero."

"Naw." Josh shakes his hand. "It's good to meet you, too. I'm sorry I didn't meet you at the barbecue."

"No sweat. You're meeting me now. I'm glad someone around here is keeping my little sister out of trouble."

"I don't need anyone to keep me out of trouble," I interrupt.

"Oh, you do so," he counters.

"Hey, I was going to invite Chris to go out to dinner with me tonight," Josh tells him. "You should come with us."

Zack smiles at him. "I'd love to, but I gotta get back to my business. Thanks for the invitation. Maybe next time."

They shake hands and my brother kisses me on the cheek. "I love you. I'll see you soon."

"Bye," I tell him. "I love you, too."

He gives me a hug, and just before he pulls away, he whispers in my ear, "Congratulations. I'm happy for you."

He lets me go, beams at me once, and heads out to his car.

Josh goes back to helping Danny unload the new gear. Josh doesn't say anything else about inviting me to go out to dinner with him, but Danny definitely heard the whole conversation.

I go back inside the training room and go on with my workday. Josh catches up with me in the locker room just as I'm getting ready to leave. "So?" he tells me.

I look up and then look around me. "So?"

"So....will you go out to dinner with me?"

I burst into a huge, blushing smile. "I'd love to."

He grins back. "So can I pick you up around seven-thirty?"

I can't help laughing. "Oh, so we're doing this by the book, are we?"

"Damn right. I wouldn't do it any other way."

"Okay, Beaver. I'll see you there. Do you need the address?"

"I already have that. John gave me the firehouse phone list, remember?"

I turn bright red and shut my locker. "Oh, yeah. I guess I won't be able to hide from you now."

"Not unless you go on the run." He squeezes my elbow. "See you in a few hours."

I go home feeling giddy. I didn't sleep here last night because.....well.....

I keep getting butterflies while I take a shower and change to get ready to go on a date with Josh. That sounds so crazy—going on a date.

I can't help my nerves as seven o'clock passes and seven-thirty creeps closer. I check my appearance in the mirror a thousand times.

I'm wearing another ruffle skirt over my biker shorts with a white blouse. I select a tailored white blazer instead of my denim jacket.

I smooth my hair down and jump a foot in the air when Josh knocks on my door. I raced over there and try to act nonchalant when I open it.

He looks stunning in a casual charcoal-grey suit with no tie and polished black leather shoes. He looks amazing in his Fire Department uniform, too, but this is a side of him I've never seen.

I blush and grin at him. "Hi."

His cheeks color. "Hi. You look delicious."

I giggle. "So do you."

"Let's wait until after the main course, okay?" he teases. "The other patrons might have heart attacks."

I laugh and he leads me out to his truck, opens the door for me, and shuts it when I get into the passenger seat.

He drives into town and keeps shooting me grins on the way. "Your brother seems like a good guy."

"He is....and he's really protective, so you better watch out."

Now it's his turn to laugh. "Thanks for the warning. Just telling you my mom is really protective, too."

"I saw pictures of her at your house. She looks really nice."

"She is—as long as you treat me right."

I have to laugh along with him. "She might get territorial if she finds out I'm moving in on you."

He glances over at the next stop light. "Is that what you're doing?"

"I just meant after your recent heartbreak. She might decide you're too fragile...."

He bursts out laughing. "I'm sure she couldn't possibly hate you more than she hates my ex."

"I'll bet she does."

"What about your brother? Does he hate your ex?"

"If, by hate, you mean, did my brother swear to spend every penny he has to hunt the guy down and tear his arms off, then yes, my brother hates my ex."

Josh winces. "Ouch."

"Fortunately, Zack hasn't found him yet. He's probably living the life of Riley in the Bahamas or something with his forty-foot yacht and his....." I trail off. "Sorry. I don't want to spend our evening talking about that."

"You're right. I shouldn't have brought it up." He steers into the restaurant parking lot. "We're here."

He opens the door for me again to get out of the truck. Then he grins when he offers me his arm to escort me inside. I guess we're doing this the official way.

The maître d' gives us a nice, quiet table in the corner, which is a good thing because the restaurant is crowded. It's much nicer than I expected and I cringe when I see the prices on the menu.

I don't argue, though. If this is what Josh wants, then I'll go along with it. I feel like I should be offering to pay for my meal, but he's been acting so official and gentlemanly that I don't say anything.

I try to choose something not too expensive. The waiter takes our orders, and when he leaves, Josh extends his hand across the table to take mine. "Hi," he tells me.

I blush again. "Hi."

"I gotta ask," he blurts out. "What did you think of me when we met on that first call?"

"What do you think I thought?" I counter. "Why do you want to know that?"

"I just want to know your first impression. It wasn't the way I usually meet women."

I turn bright red and laugh nervously. "It isn't the way I usually meet guys, either."

"So what did you think? Did you think I was a prick for telling everyone what to do?"

"Of course not!" I exclaim. "Why would you assume that?"

"Because so many other people on the fire crew thought I was a prick for telling everyone what to do."

"Actually, no one thought that on the call itself," I tell him. "They only said that after they found out you were coming to work with us as Ellen's replacement. Before they found that out, they all thought you were great for being so competent."

"Is that what you thought?"

"What—that you were competent?"

"Yes," he replies.

"I didn't think you were competent. I thought you were one of the most impressive paramedics I'd ever worked with—probably *the* most impressive paramedic I'd ever worked with. I was floored by the way you handled yourself and everything and everyone else. I was amazed. I thought you were better than great."

He beams at me across the table. "Thanks."

"Why would you ask that? Why do you think I defended you when you first came to work at the firehouse?"

"I don't know. That's why I'm asking."

I shake my head. "I knew that first day that you were going to work out. That call convinced me that you knew exactly what you were doing and that you were perfectly well qualified to take Ellen's place."

"Weren't your other hires?"

"God, no!" I exclaim. "Not by a million miles. The ones that were competent didn't fit in with our culture. They didn't like it and they left."

"That sucks."

"You aren't doubting yourself, are you?" I ask. "You aren't doubting your place on the crew, are you?"

"Not on the crew. I was asking to find out about you."

I squeeze his hand. "You don't have to worry about that."

He beams at me. "Would you like to know what I thought of you when I first met you on that call?"

"Um.....I'm not sure I want to know."

"I thought—in addition to everything you just said about me being the most impressive paramedic I'd ever worked with—I thought you were by far the most beautiful paramedic I've ever laid eyes on. I thought you were stunning—and it was delightful to see the way you handled Emily on her first day. She really got lucky when John assigned you as her training officer."

I lower my eyes to the table and my cheeks burn. "Thanks."

He rubs his thumb across my knuckles. "And I feel like I got really lucky to have you moving in on me. This is perfect."

I laugh, but before I can reply, someone comes up to our table. I expect it to be the waiter or the maître d'.

I'm too stunned to react right away when my ex-fiancé drops onto one knee by the table, places his hand on my forearm right above where I'm holding Josh's hand, and my ex moves his face close to mine.

He's wearing the exact same suit he had on the last time I saw him—the day he walked out on me. He's too dim even to realize the irony.

"Chris! I've been looking everywhere for you!" he exclaims. "I've been going out of my mind trying to find you!"

I grimace in disgust and tear my arm out of his grasp, but I have to pull my hand away from Josh when I do it. "Get away from me, Baxter," I tell him. "I don't know how you found me here, but I don't ever want to see you again."

"Give me a chance to explain!" he breathes. "We can work this out."

"There's nothing to work out," I snap. "Stand up, walk out of here, and don't come near me again."

"Why—so you can go on a date with *this* loser?" Baxter wrinkles his nose at Josh.

"You're the loser, Baxter," I growl. "What's the matter? Did Tatiana dump you? I hope she took all your money while she was at it."

Baxter shoots to his feet and glares down at me. "I came all this way to see you. You might at least give me some consideration. Who's this jackass, anyway?" He waves at Josh again. "I'm sure he can't be as good for you as I am."

"Who he is is none of your business, Baxter!" I fire back. "You disappeared out of my life three years ago. You have no business showing up here now to ruin my life for the second time."

Baxter doesn't listen. He turns to Josh. "Well? What makes you so great that you deserve a quality woman like Chris? What do you do for a living, anyway?"

"I'm a firefighter," Josh replies without a trace of hesitation.

Baxter snorts. "How much do you make a year? I bet you don't even own your own house."

"Baxter!" I snap. "Shut up and get out of here. If you doxed my phone to find out where I was, I'll report you to the Police and get you arrested."

Baxter ignores me again. "I cleared five million last year," he tells Josh. "Chris lived in a penthouse in downtown Portsmouth before she moved up here. Did you know that? I made CFO of my company before I turned twenty-five. What have you done?"

"Baxter—that's enough!" I hear my voice rising and a few other patrons turn around to stare at us.

Josh doesn't react at all. He leans back in his seat and waves at me. "Go on, man. Take your best shot. If you can convince Chris to go with you, I'll be happy for you. I won't stand in your way."

I stare at him in shock. Wow. I was impressed with him before, but now I know he's something really special. Baxter's money and accomplishments don't threaten Josh at all.

Baxter stares at Josh, too. Then Baxter glances over at me.

I know the guy too well not to read the thoughts going through his mind. He's so deluded that he really thinks he can convince me to give him another chance.

He goes down on one knee again, takes my hand, and lowers his voice to a sultry murmur. "Chris—I love you. I always have. You're the woman of my dreams. I know we've had our problems in the past, but we can work all that out. I doubled my salary last month and I bought a big apartment in Manhattan. You don't have to work anymore. I'll take care of everything. You know we belong together. No one else can give you the life you deserve." He puts his hand into his inner jacket pocket, pulls out a black velvet box, and cracks it open in front of me. "Will you marry me? I can't live without you."

A bunch of people at nearby tables who've been listening to us burst into applause as he finishes. Whistles break out in the restaurant and someone calls, "Congratulations, man!"

I stare down at a huge engagement ring tucked into the velvet box's satin lining. The center stone is massive, ostentatious, and probably cost a fortune.

I can't think why on God's green Earth Baxter would think this would convince me. He must think I'm either irretrievably stupid or hopelessly desperate to take him back because I have nothing else going in my life.

Those two assumptions on their own would be enough to make me kick him in the teeth, but the fact that he wants me to quit working as a paramedic seals the deal.

He obviously doesn't know a thing about me. He has no clue how much my work means to me. He wouldn't suggest I give it up if he did.

I wait for the applause to die down before I get to my feet, raise my voice, and call out to the whole restaurant—now that everyone is listening to us.

"You all might like to know that this man left me for another woman, broke my heart, and ruined my life." Dead silence falls over the restaurant. I point to Josh. *"This* man saved my life twice—once when I got attacked in a parking lot and again when we both got trapped in a burning building. He's a true hero. If I'm ever able to marry anyone after this piece of trash destroyed my life, I'll marry this man—not some lowlife jackass with a fat wallet who thinks it's okay to stomp my heart into the dirt, stalk me, and come crawling back expecting me to forget what he did. You can leave now, Baxter. We're done here."

I sit down. Josh bursts into another massive grin, picks up my hand, and kisses my knuckles. More people cheer and someone throws their napkin at Baxter.

"Get out of here, you piece of shit!" someone calls. "You can return the ring and get a full refund."

Baxter turns a darker shade of red, glares at me, and snarls, "This isn't over, Chris."

"It sounds an awful lot to me like it is," Josh tells him.

Baxter pretends not to hear. He glares at me for another minute and then strides out of the restaurant.

I steal a sidelong peek at Josh over our water glasses, but he keeps beaming at me from ear to ear. His cheeks glow with pleasure, but just then the waiter comes over with our food.

I can't stop blushing when I see the expression on Josh's face, so I look down at my plate and start eating.

Did I really say that? Did I really say I might marry Josh?

I said it and I don't want to take it back. The idea scares the shit out of me, but those words hover between us. I meant it and I don't regret saying it. Just don't ask me how I'm ever gonna work up the courage to go through with it.

Chapter 14: Chris

J osh tugs my hand to stop me in the restaurant parking lot. He turns me around to face him and closes both hands around my cheeks to kiss me.

His eyes brim with unbelievable emotion. "Thank you," he breathes.

"What for—for going out to dinner with you? I'm the one who should be thanking you after the money you just dropped on me."

"I'm talking about what you said to Baxter," he murmurs. "No one has ever stood up for me the way you have—and you just keep doing it. You've never let me down even once."

I snort. "You didn't really think I would take him back, do you?"

"I didn't think you would stick up for me the way you did." He lifts my lips to kiss me. "I don't know what to say. I'm......" He trails off.

I don't know what to say to him, either. I didn't do anything special by sticking up for him—tonight or any of the other times I've stuck up for him.

He's the best man I've ever met. Of course I stick up for him. I would never let anyone talk any shit about him. He doesn't deserve that.

"I want to take you home with me tonight," he murmurs. "I'll understand if you don't want to...."

"Of course I want to," I exclaim. "How can you even ask that? Do you know how much I want you?"

He bursts into another magnificent grin, but his eyes overflow with emotion. He almost looks like he's in pain. "I want you, too," he husks. "I've never wanted anything as much as this. It....it scares me....how I feel about you."

I want to kiss him, but that doesn't seem good enough for this moment. I put my arms around him and hug him. I just want to make everything okay for him—and for me.

We both pull back and he kisses me again. "You could come to my place," I suggest. "As long as your mom doesn't hunt me down afterward."

He bursts out laughing. "Let's not tell her."

I join in the joke. "Problem solved."

He takes my hand. "I want you to come home to my place. I have coffee there."

"You really know how to bait the trap, don't you? All right. I'm sold."

He opens the truck door and holds my hand until I sit down in the passenger seat. Then he drives me back to his place.

He holds my hand on the way inside. He leads me back through the front door, but he doesn't turn on the light.

The streetlamps outside give the living room an unearthly glow. It reminds me of our night at the beach.

He shuts the front door. It makes a loud click and he puts his keys on a table against the wall. Then he comes over to me.

His eyes gleam with the same bottomless well of emotion. He clasps his hands around my cheeks again, kisses me, and stares deep into my eyes.

The way he's looking at me makes my heart wring with unstoppable emotion, too. I don't want to look away from those eyes.

I want every night to be like it was at the beach—like it is right now. I want to feel this deep connection with him.

I just want to love him and keep pouring everything I have into him. I want to keep supporting him and showing him how incredible he is.

The instant I think that, the words come to me. I don't try to stop them. I murmur under my breath, "I love you," at exactly the same instant he says it back to me.

As soon as I say it, I know it's true. I told my brother I love him and I said it in front of Josh. I don't feel the same way about Josh that I do about my brother. I feel more for Josh than I do for my brother.

I never want this to end. I never want to lose this. I want him to know I'll always be there to stick up for him. I want him to know I'll always back him up and do everything to be there for him.

He pulls me into his arms and gives me a long, deep hug. I hold him and sink into this feeling.

He wants me to be all those things. He wants me to be the one who sticks up for him and has his back and is always there for him.

Is that what love is? If it is, then I'm all in. I'm more than glad to be all in.

I don't know what he plans to do. I don't know if he'll attack me and rip my clothes off right here in the living room, but I suppose that isn't really his style.

He keeps running his fingers through my hair, cradling my cheeks, and pulling me in for long, deep kisses.

I let go of everything else and just settle into this. I don't need to be anywhere else or for this to be anything else.

If coming home with him means these long, slow, deep, delicious kisses, then that's good enough for me. Just holding him and being in the same room with him is good enough for me.

He takes my hand, backsteps, and sits down on the back of the couch. He draws me between his knees, kisses me, rubs my arms, and wraps his arms around my waist to hold me.

Now I can put my arms around his neck and comb my fingers through his hair and touch his cheeks while we kiss. Everything we do feels right. It feels like we could keep going on with this forever. I sure wish we could.

So why can't we?

Time stops. Maybe this night will last forever.

He runs his hands up my back and then down to the curve of my waist. This vast, oceanic sensation doesn't change even when he lowers his hands to the backs of my thighs while we kiss.

He uses my thighs to pull me forward and desire floods me, but he doesn't take it any further than just holding me against him kissing me.

I don't want to feel anything but this closeness between us—this endless expanse of possibilities. The future is unwritten, but I don't need it to be written—not yet. I just want tonight.

He tugs my blazer off, but that's all. His hands feel warmer and closer through my T-shirt. They flood me with closeness for him. I love the way he touches me. Anything he does to me will be good.

He pulls his jacket off next. I feel how muscular he is through his shirt. He feels powerful and so intoxicatingly male.

He finally eases off and stares up into my eyes from below. "I want to ask you something, baby," he murmurs. "It might make you uncomfortable, but I need you to tell me the truth no matter what. Okay? If anything happens between us, I need to know the truth.

Don't sugarcoat it or hold anything back from me. Okay? Do you understand?"

I gulp and nod. "Okay. I understand."

"Do you promise to tell me the truth?" he asks. "Do you give me your word of honor you won't keep anything from me?"

I can only nod again, but my heart flips. What is he going to ask me?

He takes his hands off my body and holds both of mine in his. His eyes drill me to my core.

"I want to know if anything I did reminded you of Patrick," he breathes. "I want to know if I did anything that scared you or made you think I might hurt you. I want to know if there is anything I *could* do that might make you feel that way. Tell the truth. Don't spare my feelings."

Now my heart actually stops when I realize what he's saying. I have to look down so I don't see the way he's looking at me.

"Baby...." he prompts. "I asked you a question. You promised you would tell me."

"I know. I just...." I flounder trying to find the right words. "When we were at the beach....."

So many thoughts and feelings rush in on me. I have to sort through them to figure out what I felt that night.

He sits there staring at me and waiting for me to answer.

I have to shut my eyes completely before I can bring myself to say it. "When we were at the beach......I started to get scared when you held onto my hair.....and then......when you were on top of me......I started to think about him......but then I remembered that it was you and it was all right because I trusted you....."

"So it was all right?" he asks.

I nod and open my eyes. Just looking at him scares me. No one has ever seen me like this. I want to hide from that look, but the only place I can hide is in him.

"If I ever do anything that scares you, I want you to tell me," he goes on. "I don't want you to hide it from me."

"It doesn't....."

He silences me by placing his finger on my lips. "Just tell me. I'm depending on you to tell me. Okay? I never want you to think of me that way. Do you understand? I'm trusting you to tell me if something scares you or hurts you."

"I will," I tell him.

"So.....how do you feel about me grabbing your hair?" he asks.

"I don't mind it," I tell him.

"You don't mind it," he repeats. "Do you like it?"

My heart turns another somersault. "Yes. I like it."

His eyes dart to my hair and he trails his fingertips through it. "Did you like the way I held you at the beach?"

My lips form the word, *Yes,* but no sound comes out. I have to clear my throat to say it out loud. "I liked everything you did at the beach."

"Did you like it when I was on top of you?" he asks.

His eyes hold me spellbound. I can only whisper, "Yes."

He leans in and kisses me again. He draws me against his body, holds me, and kisses me for a long time.

I don't know what to think about that conversation. I guess it's all over and we're just going back to kissing now.

I get lost in that kiss. I don't know how long we've been here in this living room before he stands up, takes my hand, and leads me down the hall to his bedroom.

When we get there, he sits down on the edge of the bed, pulls me between his knees, and kisses me again for another eternity.

I could spend all night like this, just kissing with our clothes on. Maybe that's all he wants and that's okay with me.

I don't know how long we stand there—or I stand there while he sits. I'm content to just go along with whatever he wants to do.

He eventually scoots back on the bed, reclines against his pillows, and pulls me down onto his chest. He kisses my hair, settles me in the crook of his arm, and uses his fingertips to rake my hair back from my face again and again.

I put my arms around him and sink into his chest. If the rest of our relationship is nothing but this, I'll be satisfied with that. I just want it to be like this—us alone together in the dark. I've never felt anything as good as this.

The minutes slip away one after the other. The bliss of being with him overwhelms me, but I don't want to spend this time just lying here. I want more. Lying here isn't enough for me anymore.

I push myself up on my elbow to look down at him. He gazes up at me and pushes my hair back with his fingertips.

Overpowering emotion consumes me when I look at him like this. I want him. I want so much more than we've ever had before.

I bend down and kiss him. Kissing him feels magical and heavenly. His arm slips behind my back.

This is nothing we haven't been doing for hours, but I feel differently now. My body takes over. My body wants his body.

I kiss him more deeply, hungrily, more passionately. I want him to touch me. I want him to take me.

I caress his cheeks while we kiss, and when that isn't enough, I roll on top of him.

As soon as I get into that position, my desire erupts and I press myself down on top of him.

He matches my intensity and lets the energy rise. He strokes his hands down my waist to my hips and pulls me against his crotch. He crushes my ass in both hands, slides down to my thighs, and pulls my legs apart.

I sob and moan in his mouth and then, like something out of a distant dream, he raises his knee between my legs.

I gasp as he steers my hips onto it. I rush back to our make-out session in the parking lot and sink onto his leg as a surge of aching desire hits me.

I can't stop grinding on his leg. I try to kiss him, but I keep having to pull off in agonizing, gasping groans. Pleasure sweeps over me. I can't stop myself.

He pumps up into me from below and his hands follow every powerful rocking motion. He knows exactly how to turn me on.

His hands fly to my breasts and he squeezes and manhandles them through my T-shirt. I moan and whine in deep need. My thighs crack apart trying in every way to excite myself on his leg.

He tears away from my mouth, dives into my chest, and bites me through my shirt. I squeal as that sharp sensation spikes me into an even higher state of frenzy.

I grab his head, but he's already stripping up my T-shirt, pulling it over my head, and unclipping my bra.

I grab at his shoulders, but his shirt stops me from touching him. I want him like never before.

He pulls my bra off and my breasts fall into his greedy, devouring mouth. I scream and drive myself down harder on his leg, and before I can move, he crams his hand between my thighs and thrusts his fingers inside me.

I scream even louder as a torrential orgasm rockets me out of my mind. I scream again and again hurling myself onto his fingers. His mouth locks on my breast and sends lightning bolts of sensation blasting through me.

Before I can recover or even stop moaning in ecstasy, he hooks his arm around my waist, rears off the bed, and flips me onto my back.

He lays me on the bed, pulls down my skirt, shorts, and panties in one expert move, yanks off his shirt, and falls onto his hands and knees over me.

He kisses me and I get lost in his lips, but when I raise my arms to put them around his neck, I feel the bare skin of his shoulders, back, and chest against my skin.

His heat floods me with another tidal surge of rapturous desire. I want to wrap my whole body around him and feel his strength pumping into me from every inch of my skin in contact with his skin.

He attacks my mouth and my body writhes in hungry passion underneath him. I'm naked with my own juices staining my thighs. I feel smoking hot and on fire for him. I want him to see and feel me burning up with this insatiable need for him.

I touch him all over his back, neck, shoulders, and chest. I want to touch every part of him, but he's kissing me too fast.

He uses his mouth to push my face aside, gnaws across my cheek to my neck, and starts working his way down my body with hot, wet, biting kisses.

I squeal and moan every time he drops one of those blistering kisses on my skin. Everything he does makes my skin ultra sensitive. I almost feel like I could climax just from him kissing me.

He holds himself up on his arms and works his way down to my breasts. He leaves me whimpering in agony as he glides down my stomach with brutal slowness.

He takes his time kissing my thighs, pushing them apart, and then burying his face in me. I shriek and try to buck against his mouth, but he takes his time and teases me to the height of passion.

He pins my thighs down, skewers his fingers into me to make me scream, and then cups my ass to lift me into his mouth.

He breaks off long before I've had enough. I lie spasming and sobbing on his bed. I need him so bad. He drives me crazy.

He crawls back up to my mouth and doesn't try to do anything more than kiss me. He stays on his hands and knees like he just wants to stay there forever.

I wrap my arms around his neck and my legs around his waist. I try everything to pull him down on top of me, but he doesn't budge.

He stares at me with those huge brown eyes. He sees exactly what he's doing to me. He sees how much I ache for him, but he still doesn't give in.

I'm on the brink of desperate tears when he shifts his weight, takes hold of one of my wrists, and steers my hand down between his legs. He places my hand on his hot, hard, throbbing package.

He feels amazing in there and I squeeze. His eyes clamp shut for a split second and he lets out one gasping breath through his nostrils while we kiss. His eyes tell me so much. He wants this. He wants me to touch him.

I rub and squeeze him through his pants and then, very slowly, I start to unbuckle his belt.

He stares at me while I unzip him and dart my hand down his pants. I massage him through his underwear. That aching gasp of pleasure and desire makes me want him even more. He sounds amazing like this.

I want to make him feel so good. I want him to enjoy this as much as I do.

I stroke him through his underwear for a few minutes while we kiss and then I sneak my hand all the way inside. He throbs and spasms in my hand. Every stroke makes him gasp and catch his breath. I love that sound.

I caress him all along his length and pull him up so his shaft can grow to its full thickness. I burrow down to his balls, squeeze them, and then come back to his shaft.

I love how hard and strong he feels. That thick rod is what's going to take me to the stars. I don't have to doubt that. I want everything that thing can give me. I want it hard, strong, and unstoppably male and hot.

I push his pants down and he kicks them away along with his shoes. Now he's as naked as I am, but he still doesn't lower himself onto me.

I stroke him some more, but that doesn't seem to be enough. This powerful, veiny slab of meat in my hand needs more and I need more of it.

I tighten my grip and stroke him harder as I break away from his mouth and crawl my way down his neck. I keep up the same rhythm with my hand while I bite his ears and down his neck to his chest.

I keep inching down the bed underneath him, kiss him all over his chest and stomach, and eventually work my way down to his crotch.

I guide him into my mouth from below and savor those deep, shuddering gasps as he starts to stroke into my mouth. I want him to feel the pleasure and sensation he gave me.

His body quakes and strains all over. "Jesus, baby!" he whispers and starts panting hard. "Oh, fuck."

I love hearing how much he wants it. I let my hands caress his chest and stomach and even his face while he glides deep into my mouth, but pretty soon, he pulls away by himself.

I take the hint and crawl back up to his mouth. I take my time to kiss his stomach, chest, and neck on my way back to kissing him.

He lowers himself just enough for his tip to touch my enflamed tissues. I wrap my legs around him and angle my hips just enough to envelop him.

He groans again, and this time, he lets all his weight fall against that deep, hot thrust. He drills it into every excruciating inch of me and makes me seethe in blistering ecstasy as he fills me to the breaking point.

I thrash underneath him as the intensity of sensation takes over. Every thrust drives me wild with overwhelming pleasure and power.

He arches his back and screws all the way in with masterful strokes. I shriek and claw at him trying to cope with it all. He's killing me with so much pleasure. I can't stand it, but I have to.

He kisses me and his lips consume me in an endless delirium of magical bliss. I match his rhythm as he picks up speed.

I whine and moan, but he's already giving me everything I want and need. I don't want any more, but he escalates even higher and blasts me out of this world all over again.

He builds to a driving, pounding, jackhammering thump that destroys my resolve. I succumb to a screaming wreck as one wave of bliss follows another. I can't take this.

Before I can think twice, he pulls out, scoops one arm under me, and rolls me onto my stomach. His hot skin covers me from behind and he dives in to kiss me over my shoulder.

He bites my neck and then crawls his greedy, devouring mouth across my cheek to my mouth. I have to arch backward to meet that kiss.

As soon as I do, he pushes my legs apart with his knees, crushes me into the mattress, and plunges into me from behind and below.

I scream as the sensation sends me reeling into another dizzy tornado of pleasure and overpowering intoxicated desire.

I lose contact with his mouth, but he only attacks me more furiously as he starts arching into me from behind.

He drills me into the mattress even harder, but this position releases some animal passion in me I didn't know was there.

I bare my teeth and snarl trying to get every inch of him inside me. I want him to conquer me and destroy me with his power. I've never felt anything like this and I want it.

Without warning, his fingers snake into my hair, clench into a fist, and he pulls my head up and back.

I gasp, but this is nothing like I experienced with Patrick or at the beach. This is pure, raw, untamed madness unleashed from the very bottom of my soul.

He sinks his teeth into my neck and then my cheek, but I'm panting, snarling, and gasping too fast to even think of kissing him. This deep resounding beat of his body against mine is everything I've ever wanted and more.

I feel myself spiraling into another dimension. He's taking me there. He's the one giving me this.

He doesn't wait for me to get used to that before he shoves his powerful arms under me, lifts me off the mattress, and pulls me upright. He can't hold onto my hair like this, but I don't care. Anything he does to me will be good. It will be better than good. It will be amazing.

I submit to everything as he rises on his knees and sits me on his lap. I straddle him facing away, but his arms guide me exactly where he wants me. He doesn't leave me to do it myself.

He holds me against him through the whole move, and as soon as I get into that position, his arms guide me in the same deep, booming rhythm that destroys everything else.

He scrapes one powerful hand up my chest, crushes my breast for an instant, and then scoops up my neck to grip my jaw. He uses that hand to pull my head back against him.

That one extra inch of arching backward angles my body exactly where he can pound me to oblivion. I scream endlessly as one spiking climax after another consumes me. He doesn't stop. He just keeps delivering these devastating blows that blast me out of my mind.

I dissolve in his arms. I'm what he wants me to be and that over-powers me with the greatest ecstasy of my life.

I hear him grunting with the effort as his own energy builds to a release. His hands clamp on me tighter to bring me against him the way he wants me to, but everything he does blows me out of my mind until I can't take any more.

I can always take more of this. I don't know where this will stop, but I will always want more. The more he does, the more I want.

The tighter he clamps his arms and hands around me, the more I want him to mold me and maneuver me where he wants me.

I want him to control my position and take me places I never thought possible. I want him to do all of that and take me as his own. I can't imagine anything more blissful than that.

Chapter 15: Josh

I wake up with my arms around Chris's naked body and immediately shut my eyes so I can preserve this feeling. I don't want to move in case I wake her up.

She feels heavenly in my arms like this with her naked back pressed against my chest and her bare ass tucked against my hips.

All the memories of last night come rushing back. She's everything I could ever wish for and more.

One memory stands out above the rest—the words she said to Baxter at the restaurant. *He's a true hero. If I'm ever able to marry anyone after this piece of trash destroyed my life, I'll marry this man.*

She said that about me. If she marries anyone, it will be me.

God, I love her! I want to marry her right now—today. I want to drive her into town, take her to the county courthouse, and never let her go home to her place ever again.

I want to feel her sleeping in my arms like this all the time. I just want....this. I want to bury my face in her hair right now, but that might wake her up and spoil the moment.

We both have to work today. She doesn't have her uniform, which means I need to drive her back to her house to get it.

All the more reason why I need to marry her so that doesn't happen again. She should be here with all her stuff. Then she can go take a shower and get dressed while I make her morning cappuccino.

I smile to myself thinking about it. This woman—I'll never let her go—not ever.

I shut my eyes and sink into all those beautiful memories. I love the way her body moves in my arms. I love the way she rides my leg and shows me so plainly how much she needs me. I love that she wants me that much. She can get off on anything I do no matter what it is.

I'm just starting to drift off when she stirs. I'm still floating in a dream world when she screws her hips back into me and rotates her ass trying to get me to wake up and take her again.

She finally twists onto her other side, but I'm too dopey even to kiss her.

She kisses my face and down my neck whining in animal desire. She's insatiable.

She glides one silky thigh over my leg and rubs herself against me. She's already slippery with wetness and she smears her wetness on my leg.

Her sighs rise to mewing noises and she finally bucks against me screaming in my ear. My hands take on a life of their own tracing her magnificent curves, rubbing her ass and breasts, and I inhale the sweet scent of her drifting into my nose.

She finally collapses back on the pillow sobbing with the last throes of ecstasy. Mmmm. I could get addicted to that sound.

I open my eyes and gaze at her face all glowing with rapture and exhaustion. Her drunken eyes float open to meet mine and she coughs. "Sorry," she husks.

"Don't apologize. You can move in on me anytime you want to."

She smirks, blushes, and her eyelashes dip. Beautiful.

I kiss her. She feels all soft and rubbery and pliable. I want to pull her in and make her scream again, but just then, the alarm goes off on my phone.

I have to roll away and dig it out of my jacket pocket to turn off the alarm. I usually leave the phone on the bedside table where I can reach it.

When I pull my phone out, I see a notification from Chief Brewer. I tap it and read the message.

"What's going on?" Chris asks.

"It's a message from Chief Brewer. Leila is still at the hospital and Keith is with her. The chief has to reshuffle the schedule again. He wants to know if I'll work on the ambulance with Drew. He's calling in Sophie to partner with you on the rescue truck."

She runs her hand up my back. Holy shit, that touch feels good!

"Is Leila all right?" she asks.

"Hold on. I'll ask him."

I sit up and send the text back telling him the change in schedule is no problem.

He writes me back right away. "He says she isn't in labor yet. They're just doing some tests to make sure the contractions aren't anything dangerous. He says he and Danny are assuming she's fine until they hear otherwise. Then he thanks us for asking and he says he'll see us at work."

She snickers. "You mean he says he'll see *you* at work. He doesn't know I'm here."

I put the phone down and roll over to kiss her. I want to do more, but we both have to go to work.

I comb the hair out of her eyes and gaze at her angelic face. "Come over here again tonight. Come over every night. In fact, stay here forever."

She laughs and wraps her arms around my neck to pull me down on top of her. "You're so sweet."

"Is that a yes?" I ask.

"Let's have that conversation with our clothes on, okay?"

I sink into her kiss and then we get on with the business of getting up, showering, and eating breakfast before work.

I head for the kitchen while she showers and fire up the espresso machine. I go into another fantasy about sneaking into the shower with her. One of these days.....

I drive her to her house and drop her off in plenty of time for her to change into her uniform, organize her gear, and drive to the firehouse. I get there almost an hour early so no one notices us showing up at the same time.

Drew shows up and the two of us start checking out the ambulance. By the time we finish, Chris is already on the clock and deep into doing her own checks on the rescue truck.

She talks to Sophie and Danny about Leila. Drew and I are too busy to join their conversation.

We're just finishing our checks when Chief Brewer shows up. Everyone mobs him for information about Leila, but before he can say anything, we get a call-out.

I jump in the ambulance with Drew. He drives while I check the dispatch notes.

"We got a car accident on the highway!" I tell him over the sirens. "One unconscious patient. No other cars or casualties involved."

He shoots me a grin from the driver's seat. "Boring!"

I chuckle, but we don't have time to say anything else before we get to the scene.

The Police wave the rescue truck into position. Danny, Billy, Caleb, and Ellis jump out to secure the vehicle. It lies on one side with the female driver hanging sideways from her seatbelt. Her hair hangs over her face.

Then Chris and Sophie move in to check the patient. Drew and I wait for them to bring the patient over. The patient could be in any condition from a bad concussion to near death. We won't know until we see her.

The crew takes a long time to extricate the patient, secure her to a backboard, and load her onto a gurney. Chris and Sophie aren't doing compressions or intubating or even setting up an IV. The patient must not be too critical.

The two paramedics don't call me and Drew to come and help them, either. The guys wheel the gurney over to the ambulance.

"What do we got?" I ask Chris.

"Massive contusion to the right side of her head, but no instability or other signs of fracture. Everything else looks good apart from being unconscious. All her vital signs are normal."

"Got it. We'll take her from here."

I move over to the gurney and freeze when I look down at the patient. It's my ex-fiancé, Lena.

I stop dead in my tracks and the guys wheel the gurney past me to the ambulance. I'm still standing there in shock when they load her into the unit.

"Josh!" Danny yells. "Are you okay?"

I shake myself out of my trance and hop into the back. "I'm good. Let's go."

They slam the doors and Drew pulls away. I grab my stethoscope and start taking Lena's vitals, but Chris is right. Lena is stable.

Drew pulls onto the highway and hits a pothole in the road. The ambulance bounces and Lena drifts back to consciousness. Her eyes dart around the ambulance. "Help me!" she screams. "Help me!"

I touch her hand. "Take it easy. You're okay. You got in a car accident. You're in an ambulance on the way to the hospital."

Her eyes swivel over to me, but she can't turn her head while she's secured to a backboard. She looks at me and her features twist in despair. "Josh?!"

"I'm right here." I squeeze her hand again. "You're in Howe. I'm working here as a paramedic now."

"I know!" she howls. "I came up here to find you. I .....I love you! I just want to get back what we had before. I'm sorry I left the way I did. I didn't know what to do after Chris died. I couldn't think straight. That's why I had to leave. Can't we just work it out and find a way to be together again?"

I stare at her in mounting horror when I realize what she's saying. I force myself to look down at my clipboard. "Let's get you to the hospital and get your head checked out before we have that conversation."

I have a flashback to this morning. Chris....in my bed......*Let's have that conversation with our clothes on, okay?*

Are we going to have that conversation—about Chris staying at my place always—or are we going to have the conversation about me and Lena getting back together?

"I know I messed up," Lena whimpers. "Please forgive me. You're the best thing that ever happened to me. I was stupid not to see that. Can't we just put it behind us and start over?"

"I just told you we aren't having that conversation now when you're injured in the back of an ambulance."

Just to make sure she gets the message, I move up to the jump seat behind her head and tell Drew to get me the medical team on the radio.

I give them the rundown on the call and our ETA. By the time I finish, Drew is already backing into the loading dock.

The medical team comes out and I hand off Lena to them. Then Drew and I clean up the ambulance, remake the sheets and blankets on the gurney, and I contact dispatch to tell them we're clear of the hospital.

We're just heading out to the ambulance to leave when the other ambulance comes in with two more patients. Theo Gough from the other EMS crew tells me that the two trucks and most of the crew are out at a multi-casualty warehouse disaster west of town.

Drew drives us to the address. Chris, Sophie, Andy, and Naomi are working their tails off pulling patients out of the wreckage of a partially demolished building.

Drew and I spend the next five hours treating and transporting patients. We're still doing it at the end of the shift and we all keep working late into the afternoon.

The second shift drives out in their personal vehicles to help us, but it still takes hours to get all the patients to the hospital.

Vince Jaeger pushes his car keys into my hands. "Take my car back to the station and go home. We'll take over here."

"Thanks, man," I tell him. "Are you sure you don't want me to stick around?"

"Get out of here!" he snaps. "You've been out here all day. We can finish up without you."

I start to turn away when Chris comes up to me smiling. "Can I catch a ride with you?"

I can't deal with her right now—not with Lena in the same town as me asking for us to get back together.

I hand her Vince's keys. "You take the car. I'll find my own way back to town."

I walk off alone down the highway on my way back to town. I feel her eyes boring into me from behind as I walk away and leave her standing there stunned, but I don't turn around. I need to think and I can't do that with her around.

Chapter 16: Josh

I turn onto my street heading for my house. My truck is still at the firehouse, but I see right away that I won't be able to hide from this any longer.

Chris's car sits parked at the curb. She sits on my doorstep waiting for me.

I left the warehouse scene more than three hours ago. It's taken me that long to walk here, so she's probably been sitting here waiting for me all that time.

I don't want to deal with her, but I owe her some explanation. I can't believe our night of bliss is ending like this. I can't believe all the happiness I felt this morning is now a thing of the past.

Am I really going to give all that up to get back together with Lena?

I don't know what to say to Chris, but I would be a bald-faced coward if I walked away from her right now. I have to face her and at least tell her what's going on.

I walk down the street, up the walk, and stop at a safe distance from the porch. I plant myself in front of her. Since when am I keeping all this distance between us?

I hate myself for doing it, but I can't go near her until I decide what to do about all of this. I don't know what I'm doing—with anything.

Chris doesn't say anything. She just stares at me and waits for me to say something. She doesn't make it easier for me and why should she when I'm the one shutting her out?

Am I shutting her out? If I get back together with Lena, then I will have to shut Chris out—forever.

I'm the one who said I didn't want anything casual. I'm the one who said I only wanted to get involved if it was going to be serious.

Now it is and I'm the one who's pushing her away. *Am* I pushing her away? I don't even know.

She blinks up at me with those big, soft, understanding eyes of hers. If she only knew.

I have to look away, so I glance down the street. "That woman....the woman in the car accident this morning......she's my fiancé—my ex-fiancé. She came up here to find me. She wants to get back together. She said she wants to work it out and put it behind us."

"What did you tell her?" Chris asks.

I look down at the sidewalk and kick an invisible stone away. "I told her we'd have that conversation when she wasn't injured in the back of an ambulance."

She stares at me for a second and then stands up. "Then it sounds like you need to have that conversation before you talk to me again."

She walks off to her car, gets into it, and drives away. I should stop her. I should tell her right here and now that I don't want Lena back—that I only want Chris.

I can't say that when I don't know what I want. This whole nightmare is throwing me for a loop.

I can't go into my house. Chris is right. I can't do anything until I know what I'm dealing with.

I walk away and take an hour to get back to the firehouse. I get in my truck and drive around town for another hour before I stop in front of the hospital.

I don't want to talk to Lena, but my whole future hinges on clearing the air with her. I don't know how I feel about her.

I've spent so long coping with her leaving me. I mean, it hasn't really been that long. It's only been a few months, but it feels like an eternity.

I spent so much of that time wishing she would come back. Then I spent more time hating her for not coming back and for leaving in the first place.

Now Chris is in my life—at least, she was. Lena could have stolen that from me, too. Why am I even considering taking her back?

I make up my mind to dump her hard. She destroyed my life almost as much as her brother's death destroyed my life. I could have recovered from that eventually if she'd only stuck by me.

I storm into the hospital, find out which floor she's on, and fume in the elevator on my way up there. I plan on being as harsh and cruel as I can be.

Those thoughts go out the window when I walk into the room and see her sitting up in a hospital bed. She looks vulnerable and needy with part of her head bruised and swollen.

Her eyes well up with tears when she sees me walk in. "I missed you," she croaks.

"You got a funny way of showing it," I grumble.

Her hand flies to her mouth. "Are you still mad at me for leaving?"

"Mad? I'm not mad at you for leaving. You showed me your true colors. I thought I knew you, but I didn't. I know you now."

"You can't blame me for getting upset about Chris dying," she tells me.

"I don't blame you for getting upset. I got upset, too. Do you think you were the only one who got upset about Chris dying?"

"That isn't fair!" she cries. "I never blamed you for Chris's death."

I grit my teeth to stop myself from blowing up at her completely. "Blame me! How dare you?! Chris's death destroyed me and then you walked out on me when I needed you. I loved him like a brother. Don't you give me a sob story about how messed up you were over Chris's death. I can promise you that you weren't more messed up than I was."

She compresses her lips to hold back sobs, but her tears still streak down her cheeks faster than she can wipe them away. "I'm sorry! I just want us to be together again. I'm sorry I left the way I did. Can't you forgive me for that? We were going to get married. If we were married, we would have to forgive each other for a lot of things that both of us did wrong. Can't we just start doing that now?"

"If we were married, I would need to be able to rely on you to support me and help me deal with bad shit that happens. Bad shit is always happening in my job, but I never told you because I wanted to protect you. If I can't count on you to help me through something like this, how can I count on you to help me through anything else? If we start now, then you've already shown me how you're going to deal with anything that goes wrong. You're going to run off and abandon me just to make it easier for yourself."

She bursts into tears. I used to think she looked beautiful when she cried. Now she just looks ugly, selfish, and totally oblivious to the agony and despair she's put me through these last few months.

"I'm sorry!" she wails. "I know I made the wrong call. I know I hurt you and I can't tell you how sorry I am. I would do anything to take it back. Just tell me what I have to do to make it up to you."

I don't answer. I don't know what to say to her that I haven't already said.

"You're the only person who understands!" she goes on. "No one else gets it because no one else knew him. We can't lose that. It's bad enough that we lost him. We can't lose each other, too."

Those words shatter my resolve. She's right. The worst part of losing her was losing the one other person who knew and cared about Chris the way I did.

Plenty of people offered their support and understanding about me losing my best friend. Their sympathy and understanding didn't mean shit because they didn't know him like I did—like she did.

As soon as she says that, she buries her face in her hands sobbing hard. I can't see her like this. She's crying because she lost me. She still cares.

I sit down on the edge of the bed, but that doesn't bridge the gap. I put my arms around her and she falls against me crying on my shoulder. I'm all she has...and she's all I have.

My mind goes back to the night at the beach. Chris. She understood. She might not have gone through something like I did, but she knows. She's a paramedic on the fire crew.

She never told me why those burn victims got to her. I don't have to ask. Every paramedic has something like that in their past—some patient that haunts them.

My friend is mine. I went through the same thing in the burning building when I thought she was going to die.

I unwrap my arms around Lena. I still feel something for her. That's the problem. I still care about her, too, but I can't say anymore that she's the only one who understands.

Chris understands in a way that Lena never could—and Chris has always been there for me. She never withdrew from me to protect herself.

She's put herself on the line for me time and again. She's stood up to her whole crew to defend me.

I can't be around Lena anymore. I can't think clearly even when I'm away from her.

I walk out of the hospital, get in my truck, and start driving. I don't know where I'm going until I wind up at the beach. I just want to be alone where I can think. I can't be around anyone until I figure out what I'm going to do about this.

I walk out onto the sand and walk for miles heading east. I pass the headland and sit down on the rocks to stare out at the surf.

Why did Lena have to come back now—after I already found someone else? Why couldn't she have come to her senses a week afterward or even a month afterward?

Did she have some reason to come back? Did she leave me for another man the way Baxter did and now she's coming back because that relationship ended?

I'll never know for certain. Those questions will always nag me. That's the problem. I never questioned anything about our relationship before her brother died. Now I question everything about it.

I stand up to walk back to my truck. I'm just about to get into the cab when another car pulls into the parking lot.

Chris's expression goes blank when she sees me. She parks and sits in the driver's seat with the engine running while she stares at me. Is she thinking of driving off and leaving me alone? Isn't that what I want?

I can't let her think that, so I walk around to the driver's door and spin my hand around to tell her to open the window. She does it, but she doesn't switch off the motor.

"Could you come out here, please, and take a walk with me?" I ask her. "I need to talk to you."

She studies me like she really needs to think about it, but in the end, she shuts down the engine and gets out. "Let's go," she tells me.

We start walking. We went west the night we spent out here together, so I turn east again. This way doesn't mean anything.

We walk in silence for a long time before I decide what to say to her.

"I'm sorry I left you in doubt about my intentions," I finally tell her. "That wasn't fair to you."

"What *are* your intentions?" she asks. "What conclusion did you come to from your conversation with her?"

I shrug. I didn't come to any conclusion. How cowardly is that? Why can't I just rip off the band-aid and throw Lena out of my life the way I know I should?

Chris and I come to the headland and we both stop without discussing it first. We stand there in silence looking out at the surf.

"Do you remember what you told Baxter at the restaurant?" she asks. "If your fiancé can convince you and win you back, then I'm happy for you. I care about you and you deserve to be happy, even if that isn't with me. If you really think she's better for you than I am, then I want you to be with her. I'm no prize, either, I can tell you. I have my own baggage. I don't know what you had with her, but it must have been pretty special if you were going to marry her and have kids with her and everything. I wouldn't blame you for wanting to get that back. I won't compete for your heart. If you want her, go for it. I won't stand in your way."

A bomb goes off in my mind. Of course.

Only she could say something like that. She's always had my back no matter what. Of course she would have it now, too.

I put my arms around her and bury my face in her silky black hair. "Thank you, Chris."

She straightens up and looks at me. "You're welcome. I only want you to be happy. I would never try to keep you if it made you unhappy."

I cup her beautiful cheeks and kiss her very slowly before I can bring myself to look her in the eyes. "You're the only one I want. Thank you for talking me straight. This whole thing...." I shut my eyes and shake my head. "Her coming back just messed up my head for a while."

"You don't have to explain."

I take a step back and clasp both her hands. "I'm going back to the hospital to break it off with her for good. After I do that, I won't see her again. If you'll let me, I'd like to take you out again tonight. I don't want anything to stand in our way ever again."

She bursts into a huge smile. "I'd love that."

I cradle her face in my hands again. God, she's beautiful! "I love you. You never have to compete for my heart because you already have it. I'll pick you up at seven-thirty. Okay?"

Her whole face glows with pleasure. "Okay. I'll see you there."

I turn and walk away fast. I'd like to hold her hand and meander back to the parking lot extra slowly, but I'm too excited about shipping Lena out of my life. I have to get this over with right away so I can move on.

I hop in my truck, peel out of the parking lot, and burn rubber back to the hospital. I don't hesitate at all to ride the elevator up to Lena's room.

I don't fume this time. I'm crystal clear. My future is with Chris. Lena is my past and that's where she'll stay.

She brightens up and smiles when I walk in. She looks better when she smiles, but not even that can touch me. I already know what I have to do.

I stop at the foot of her bed. How did I ever let this woman get me so confused about what I want? How could I ever think I could work it out with her?

Her eyes dart to the door behind me. "Did you see the nurses? Do you know how long I have to stay in here?"

"We're over, Lena," I blurt out. "We can never get back together—ever. You threw our relationship away and I've moved on."

"No!" she exclaims. "You can't! We belong together!"

"Maybe we did before, but you proved to me that we don't anymore. I can never trust you again."

"No, please, Josh!" she groans. "Please give me another chance! I won't let you down. I swear it. I just needed to take some time to process what happened. You can't blame me for that."

"Taking some time to process what happened means taking some time off work or going on a vacation or changing careers. It doesn't mean dumping the person you said you were going to spend the rest of your life with. This could be the smallest thing that happens to us and your first solution was to end our relationship. Well, you ended it and now it's over because that's what you wanted. Either you never valued our relationship that much to begin with or else your judgment is so poor that I can't trust you to make decisions about our lives. Either way, you ended our relationship. We can't get it back and I don't want to. I have a life up here in Howe now. I don't want to go back to what we had before."

"No! Don't do this, Josh!" she whines and stretches out her hand to me, but she's too far away. "I can make it up to you. I know I can. We were made for each other. You know we are."

"I don't think that anymore." I make a snap decision to tell her the truth. "I met someone else. I'm going to build a future with her. Hopefully, I'll be able to...."

Her expression turns to granite. "You what?! How could you do this to me?! How could you betray me like this?!"

"Betray you?!" I fire back. "You walked out on me! You left me for no reason! You could have been out there with anyone all these months while I was dealing with Chris's death alone. Don't you dare say I betrayed you when *you* were the one who betrayed *me!*"

"Who is she?" Lena snaps. "Is she some floozy you picked up off the street? Is that it? You never cared about me if you could do this to me. I hope she gives you a disease that rots you to death!"

I narrow my eyes at her. If I ever doubted my decision, all of that disappears in a breath of wind. I never belonged with this woman. I know that now.

I lower my voice to a death snarl. "Do you really want to know who she is? She's the paramedic who got you out of your car when you crashed on the highway. You could have been dead and she could have been the one who saved your life. She saved *my* life when we got trapped in a burning building together and she's had my back every day since I moved to this town. If you ever say a word against her again, I swear to God I'll....."

I break off fighting myself under control. Why in the name of God am I even in the same room with a woman who could say things like this about Chris—and me?

Lena bursts into tears again. "I'm sorry! I can't help it! I love you! I can't stand thinking of you with someone else!"

"Well, you better start thinking of it because I've moved on. I'll never get back together with you."

She sobs openly and her lips tremble all over the place. "Please..... give me another chance....."

"No," I tell her. "You had your chance and you blew it. You showed me exactly who I was engaged to and I don't want that anymore."

I walk out of the room without another word. I feel so much better, now that I got that off my chest. Now I can look forward to my date with Chris. I don't have Lena hanging around my neck anymore.

My heart flutters when I get in my truck and drive back to my house. Whoo! I feel amazing. I feel alive for the first time in months.

I go into a whirlwind cleaning my house. I want everything to be perfect when I bring Chris back here tonight—if she lets me.

She better let me. I can think of so many things I want to do with her. There aren't enough hours in the day to do everything I want to do with her.

Chapter 17: Chris

I open my door and Josh's eyes widen when he looks down at my clothes. I'm not wearing a ruffle skirt tonight.

I'm wearing a white body-con dress that hugs every curve with white heels and gold jewelry. I know I look good and his reaction is so worth it.

"Wow," he breathes.

I turn in a complete circle and blush to my eyelashes. "Do you like what you see?"

"Yeah!" he gasps and grabs my hand. "Get out here before I attack you and tear that dress off."

I giggle on our way out to the truck. "So.....how did things go at the hospital?"

"We don't talk about that. We don't ever have to think about that ever again. It's over and done with."

"Are you sure?" I ask.

"Stop it. I wouldn't be here if I wasn't." He opens the passenger door for me to get in.

I have to be extra careful about how I move around in this dress, but I see him eyeing me appreciatively when I bend at the waist.

I catch him being extra careful not to gawk at me while he drives across town to the same restaurant. "Are you sure you want to come here again?" I ask when he leads me into the lobby.

"Are you kidding? This is my new favorite restaurant." He squeezes my hand and draws me close to him. He stares deep into my eyes. "I want to come here and remember every word you said about me."

I feel myself starting to drift into those eyes. I really want to kiss him, but right then, the maître d' shows up to take us to our table. It's the same table in the back.

Josh holds my hand across the table, rests his chin in his other palm, and beams at me across the table.

I blush and squirm in my seat. "What?"

He sighs. "Just looking."

I giggle and try to look away, but his eyes hold me spellbound. "Is anything wrong?"

"Nope. Everything's perfect."

"What do you want to talk about?" I ask.

"Huh? Oh, are we supposed to talk on these dates?"

I have to laugh. "Cut it out."

His cheeks and eyes glow when he smiles at me. "What would *you* like to talk about?"

"I guess it wouldn't really be appropriate to talk about work at the dinner table, would it?"

"Is that going to be our new rule—no talking about work at the dinner table? My dad had that rule."

I lean closer. "Tell me about your family."

"There isn't a lot to tell. We're your typical corn-fed Midwestern yokels."

"I find that hard to believe. What did your parents do for a living?"

"My dad is a high school history teacher and my mom runs a daycare center for toddlers."

I frown. "That doesn't give me a lot to go on. Do you have brothers and sisters?"

"Two brothers. One sister."

"How does everyone feel about you becoming a firefighter?"

He shrugs. "They don't understand it, but they can see that I love it, so they accept it. What about you? Do you have any siblings besides your sister and brother?"

"That's all. The two of them are the only family I have My parents died in a car accident when I was seventeen. That's when I decided to become a paramedic."

His eyes widen. "Really? That sounds terrible."

"It was. The paramedics who responded to the accident were both high out of their minds on their shift beforehand. They were so far out in space that they ran the ambulance into a tree on their way to the hospital. My parents would have survived if not for that. That's when I made the decision to become a paramedic so I could make sure that never happened to someone else."

He stares at me with his jaw on the floor. "Jesus!"

"Yeah, it was bad. That's when my sister started going off the rails. I'm the youngest, so she was twenty when it happened. Zack is the oldest and he got super-duper, ultra protective of both of us after the accident. That's why he's always coming up here to check on me."

"Wow," he murmurs. "That is one hell of a story."

"All three of us are really close because of it, but Lisa sometimes has a hard time remembering that when she's three sheets to the wind. Why did you decide to become a paramedic?"

"Actually, Chris was the one who convinced me. He decided he wanted to become a firefighter and he convinced me to do it, too.

We went through the Academy together, but I found I enjoyed the medical side of it better than fighting fires. I convinced him to start EMT training with me, and once we started, we both knew that's where we belonged. I never had another partner until after he died."

"That's cool," I exclaim. "Did his death make you question your calling?"

"Not at all. Work was the one thing that got me through it. I couldn't have made it without that. If anything, it made me recommit to it. The way he died—almost getting trapped in the building with him the way I did—and the effort I put into saving him—it all kind of confirmed for me that this really was what I wanted to do. It kind of solidified for me that I wanted to do it because my heart was really in it and not because I did it with him."

"That's cool. I mean—not that he died, but that you got that confirmation."

"Yeah, that was one good thing that came out of it." He squeezes my hand across the table. "And meeting you. That was the other good thing that came out of it. I wouldn't have met you if he was still alive."

I blush and look away. "If he was still alive, you'd be married to his sister and you would never have found out I exist."

"Exactly. I'm not saying I'm glad he died, but maybe there was a reason for it after all." He rubs his thumb across my knuckles. "I definitely wound up with the right woman."

I can't stop blushing, but just then, the waiter comes with our orders and we start eating.

Josh takes a bite and wipes his mouth with his napkin. "So is Zack going to approve of you going out with me?"

"He already does," I reply. "You heard him at the firehouse."

"I just want to make sure he doesn't spend every penny he owns to hunt me down and tear my arms off."

I laugh. "I don't think you have to worry about that. He congratulated me before he left."

His eyes fall out of their sockets again. "He did?"

"Don't tell me you didn't know. How could he not after what you did at the pool hall?"

Now it's his turn to look away. "I hope you didn't make it into something it wasn't."

"I didn't."

He turns bright red and bends over his plate.

"Why don't you take credit for all the good things you've done?" I ask. "Why don't you let people admire you for being such a good person?"

He shrugs. "I guess I can't stop thinking about all the failures I've had—and all the patients I've lost. They're the ones that really bug me."

I look down at my food and push my mashed potatoes around with my fork. "I get it."

He hesitates and then asks, "Do you want to tell me about the burn victims?"

"Not really," I mumble.

"Well, if you think it will help, you can always tell me. I'll understand."

I look up at him and I know he's right. He would understand. I definitely wound up with the right guy—just in case I didn't realize that before.

We finish our meal and get back into his truck. I expect him to drive home so we can fool around again.

Instead, he drives to a park adjacent to the beach. It isn't on the beach, but we can hear the surf from here.

He takes my hand, and when he sees me shivering, he takes off his jacket and wraps it around my shoulders. Then he leads me into the trees.

He pulls me down on a bench where we can see the moonlight shining on the ocean stretching far out to sea. It's beautiful and ghostly out there.

We hold hands in the silence. I want to ask him so many more questions—about all the things I don't know about his life.

At the same time, I want to enjoy this silence. It means so much that we can just sit here together without saying anything.

He glances down at me and I look up at him. He gazes into my eyes at close range and then kisses me.

It's a simple kiss that doesn't lead to anything. He straightens up. He's about to turn back to watching the moonlight flickering on the water.

"I bought you something...." I tell him. "I hope you don't mind."

His eyebrows shoot up. "You did? Why? I don't need anything."

"I know, but I wanted to get you something—to show you how I feel about you."

"You didn't have to do that."

"Well, I did, and if I don't give it to you now, it will just keep burning a hole in my purse until I do give it to you."

He frowns. "What is it?"

I pull my purse forward, unclip it, and take out a black velvet box. I open it in front of him.

An undecorated gold wedding band sits inside. It has no sparkly gems or diamonds—no fancy engravings—nothing. It's just plain, smooth gold in a thickness that could only suit a man.

He stares down at it in stunned silence.

"Will you marry me?" I croak. "I love you and I don't want anything to stand in our way again. I want to go all in with you and I want you to go all in with me. I want you to be a father and me to be a mother and for us to have a house and kids in school and a mortgage and afterschool soccer practice and all of that. I don't want anything less than that. I don't want us to date and see where it goes. I want us to just go all in and make it work no matter what life throws at us."

He blinks down at the ring. He doesn't move for a second.

I'm just starting to wonder if I made a drastic mistake when his eyes shoot up and lock on me. "You ruined my surprise, Chris."

I frown. "What do you mean?"

He puts his hand in his jacket pocket, pulls out a black velvet box, and cracks it open. "Will you marry me? I love you and I don't want to live without you anymore. I want you to come home with me and never leave. I don't want to take you back to your place ever again. I just want you with me. I want us to wake up together from now on, no matter what."

I blink down at the ring in the box. It's much simpler than Baxter's. This one is a plain gold ring with a single diamond clamped in the setting. It's the least ostentatious engagement ring I've ever seen, but it's beyond beautiful.

I look up into his eyes and his face blurs when tears well up in mine. "I love you!"

He dives in and kisses me. Then he takes his ring out of his box, slips it onto my finger, and sniffs back tears.

He takes the box out of my hands, closes it, and kisses the box. "I'll save this for when I'm ready to put it on."

I burst out in excited laughter. We're doing this. We're going to get married.

He puts his arm around my shoulders and hugs me against his side. "So....my place or yours?"

"Do you mean tonight or long-term?"

"I was thinking long-term."

"I think yours. You've never even seen my place and yours has an espresso machine."

He laughs with me. "We could move the espresso machine if we absolutely had to."

I beam up at him. "I really don't care where we live."

"Your place is bigger," he points out.

"Yours has a bigger yard. We'll need that when we have kids."

He turns bright red and has to turn away to stifle his own nervous giggles. "You did so not just say that."

I nudge my shoulder into him. "You're gonna be great."

He turns to look at me still blushing. "So are you."

"Your place is closer to the firehouse—and the school. The firehouse kids always hang out at each other's houses, so it makes more sense to be close to everyone else."

His hand flies to his head and he gasps out loud. "My God! I can't believe we're actually talking about this!"

I wrap my arms around him and kiss him on the neck. "You were made for this."

Chapter 18: Josh

I open the door to my house to let Chris in. I shut the door behind her, put my keys on the side table, and drape my jacket over a chair.

I don't turn on the light, though. I want to see Chris like this—the way it's been between us the last two times.

She strolls through my house looking at everything extra closely. I know what she's doing. She's moving in. She's going to come live here, marry me, and become my wife.

I love the way that sounds. My wife. I can't wait to call her that and to feel everything that goes along with it.

She saunters through the kitchen, takes a look at the espresso machine, the pictures on the shelf, and everything else.

I don't interfere. I want her to make herself comfortable here.

I go sit on the couch to wait. I can wait all night. I'm going to have a lot of years to get comfortable with her.

She stops in front of the picture of me, Chris, and Lena. I'll take it down tomorrow, put it in a box somewhere, and let it start gathering dust with the rest of my past. That's where it belongs.

Chris finally crosses the living room and sits down next to me. That tight dress makes her hips and ass curve out so nicely. I love the way she looks in that dress.

Those curves are all for me. No one sees her like this when she's wearing her uniform.

She has to sit at an angle and keep her legs together. Mmmm. Beautiful.

She kicks off her heels, tucks her legs under her, and slides over to sit next to me. I put my arm behind her on the couch back and she leans against me—just like we really are husband and wife sitting on the couch together after a long day.

I smile down at her and she beams up into my face. It was never like this with Lena. We never deliberately sat down and decided that we were going to build a future together. We just let it happen because I was her brother's best friend and we were always together anyway.

I love how deliberate this is. I love that we both know what we're doing and how serious it is.

She leans in and kisses me, but it's a simple, casual husband-and-wife kiss. It's the kiss of a couple with all the time in the world—a couple that has been together for so long that all the doubt and mystery has gone out of their relationship long ago.

She clears her throat and murmurs in an undertone. "Listen....I....I don't want it to be between us like it was between you and your ex. I mean....if you have a bad call that's bugging you, I want you to tell me. I don't want you to feel like you have to protect me from that. I want to know about it no matter how bad it is."

I look down at my lap. I should have expected this. I wanted her to tell me the ugly truth. It makes sense that she would want the same thing.

She rests her hand on my thigh. "I hope that doesn't bother you."

"Does that mean you're going to tell me about your bad calls? Is that what you're saying—that you want both of us to tell each other about our bad calls? Is that how we're starting this off?"

The color drains from her face and now she's the one who looks down. She gulps hard. "If that's what you think we should do, then yes. If that's what it takes, then I'll do it. I don't want you to feel like you have to protect me from it. I mean....."

"Do you feel like you have to protect *me* from it? Is that why you don't want to talk about it?"

"I guess I feel like you have your own bad calls and hearing about mine would only make it harder for you."

"I feel the same way about you. That's why I wouldn't tell you. It isn't because I want to keep anything from you. Is that what you want—to hear about my bad calls? You know about the call where Chris died. It doesn't get much worse than that."

She looks away again. I called her bluff.

"I don't need you to tell me," I go on. "You don't have to tell me."

She clears her throat again, but she won't look at me. "You're right. I should tell you. I shouldn't expect you to tell me about yours if I'm not prepared to tell you about mine."

"Don't tell me." I cup her chin, turn her to face me, and kiss her. "I don't want to know."

She blinks her big eyes at me. They burn with terror that she might have to tell me about whatever horror haunts her.

I don't want her to if it scares her this much, so I keep kissing her. She holds herself stiffly for a minute and then relaxes into my lips.

I devour her mouth to stop her from telling me. I don't want the memory to scare her this much. If keeping it to herself helps her, that's fine with me.

I slip my fingers into her hair and grip the back of her head, but I don't tighten my fingers into a fist. I don't want to scare her with that, either.

Our mouths open and our tongues dance in a blissful swirl of heat and sizzling electric energy. I want to consume her.

I extend my hand to touch her and graze the perfect sweep of her curved side running down to her hip. That dress invites me to explore her in new ways.

I caress down her hip to her bare thigh and then crawl up it to scoot up her dress. Her legs quiver with excitement.

I can't stop touching her. I compress her breast and the aching sob of a moan shoots a blast of heat to my crotch. I'm gonna own this woman and make her all mine. I'm going to take her in every inch of this house and then do it all over again.

She trembles when I slide my hand between her knees and push her legs apart. She whimpers in ecstasy and wraps her arms around my neck to hug me into her delicious kisses.

I circle her waist with both hands, rotate her onto my lap, and tug up her dress so she can straddle me. Now I can appreciate her stunning curves in all their glory.

Her eyes smolder under her long bangs. I follow her waist upward to her breasts, down to her thighs, and glide my hand up to the back of her neck.

She locks her drunken eyes on me and her features smolder with buried fire. Her eyelids dip very slowly and float open again.

I can't stop touching her face, hair, lips, and neck when she looks at me like that. My hands trace across her bare collarbone and down to her breasts.

She clamps her eyes shuts and moans when I squeeze them through her dress. God, she's beyond hot!

She drags her gaze back to me, kisses me once, sits back to let me touch her, and her hands rise to the buttons of my shirt.

She keeps stealing glances at me while she unbuttons each button with exaggerated slowness. The feeling of her hands working on me sends a sizzle of electricity through my skin. She wants me. Her volcanic desire radiates into me through her body.

She works her way all the way down to my waistband, pushes my shirt aside, and dives into my neck. She kisses down my neck, nudges my shirt aside, and then her hot, ravenous mouth blasts me apart when she kisses across my chest and down.

Her body erupts with so much explosive passion that I can't stand it. I run my fingers into her hair and follow her movements across my skin. I touch her as well as I can, but her dress gets in the way.

I want to touch her more, and when she straightens up to kiss me, I seize her hips and pull her in.

She blasts into a torrential frenzy of rocking against me. She won't stop touching me. Now's my chance.

I push her dress up higher and then peel it over her head. She sits in front of me in her bra and panties—so beautiful, so exposed.

I touch her faster, harder. She rubs her body all over me and bucks her hips to grind on me. Her energy skyrockets off the charts.

I flick her bra open and pull it off, but that only drives her even farther into frantic moaning, rocking, and kissing me. She rubs her bare breasts against my chest and undulates under my hands propelling herself into some kind of insanity.

She pushes my shirt aside, and the next time she tries to kiss me, I cradle her back in both hands and steer her breasts into my mouth. She screams and whines, hugs my head into her chest, and pumps her hips down hard on my crotch.

The feeling of her spiraling out of control turns me on like I can't believe. This is my woman. I'm gonna marry this woman. She's mine—all mine.

That thought blows the lid off my reserve. I want to own her. I want to conquer her and stake my claim on her. I want to make her mine so no one else will ever even look at her. I want all of this—all this satin skin and beauty—to be mine alone.

I attack my belt and zipper, rip my pants open, pull her panties aside, and guide her down on top of me.

She's already bucking so hard and so fast that nothing can stop her. She explodes in a cataclysm of spasms, screaming in my ear, and her sweet hot wet channel clamps around me.

She won't stop touching my chest, attacking my mouth, riding me hard, and throwing back her hair to roar at the ceiling. Her eyes take on a wild, glazed look. She isn't home anymore. She's somewhere else, but she's still right here with me.

I clamp my hands on her hips and grind her back and forth on my thrusts to destroy her. Her juices gush around me and make me so impossibly hard that I can't take it. I need more—so much more.

I can touch her and play with her body all I like in this position. Her breasts hang before my eyes where they tempt me to play with them and make her sob and scream even higher. Her hips give me two perfect handles to hold onto to guide her as fast or as slow as I want.

Her magnificent round ass curves on my lap and my shaft fits inside her so blissfully. I could stay in there forever, but it won't work out that way.

I lean forward and strip off my shirt. Her fingers claw at my chest.

I want to turn her onto her back so I can drill her into the couch, but when I try, I wind up lying down on my back.

She rides me into that position, and as soon as I stretch out, she sits up straight in front of me.

She arches her back and slams her hips into me with almighty force. She takes me all the way in, crushes my balls under her weight, and throws back her head in screams.

Her body sways with pleasure and wild abandon. Seeing her like this—knowing that she's finally mine—it propels me over the edge. I can't hold back.

I start to lose control and she dives for my mouth. She plasters her breasts across my chest still pounding down on me. She attacks my lips kissing me hard while she slams in harder than I ever thought possible. Her passion blows me out of the water and I explode into her.

I grab her by the hair without thinking and smash her mouth into mine. I roar into her mouth as the dam breaks and everything I am pours into her.

She's screaming too loud to care and the heat pulsating into me through her channel drains the last trace of my essence.

I shut my eyes and wait for my heart to stop pounding. Chris keeps rippling over me, rubbing her body against me, kissing my cheeks, neck, and chest, and her hair spills across my skin.

I'm too exhausted to touch her, but the feeling of her rubbing her body on top of me feels too blissful. I don't want her to stop.

She finally does, though. She lies on top of me with her silky thighs straddling my hips and her face tucked into my neck.

I start to drift off again when she rotates sideways to lie down next to me on the couch. She fits perfectly between my body and my arm. She rests her head on the cushion next to mine.

Her voice drifts into my ear from out of the darkness. "I worked in Portsmouth before I moved to Howe. Baxter and I got together there and I worked at Portsmouth Firehouse while Baxter worked his way up in his company.

"Our crew got a call when a gas main blew up inside a school. It lit the whole school on fire. Most of the buildings got torched along with everyone inside them, but about fifty kids and twenty teachers escaped into the school cafeteria. They took shelter there.

"The fire consumed the rest of the school and the cafeteria was the only safe place. We went in to get them out, but before we got near the building, another gas bubble exploded under the cafeteria and enveloped the building.

"By the time the crew got the blaze under control enough for us to go in, everyone inside had gotten burned, but they were still alive. I was one of five paramedics who went in to try to save anyone we could, but they were too badly burned. Their bodies just crumbled in my hands. The kids would dissolve into pieces when we tried to intubate. I still remember their eyes looking up at me......just begging me to save them....."

She trails off. I can't open my eyes. That story is nothing I haven't heard before. I might even have had a few calls like that myself, but I don't talk about that.

I tilt my head sideways to rest it against hers. Now I know.

"I got a call in Masterson once," I tell her. "A guy fell into a high-powered industrial shredder. He fell in up to his waist before his friends pulled him out. There wasn't much left of him below the waist. He stayed conscious for ten minutes before he flatlined on us."

She doesn't respond for a minute. I don't want to look at her. I don't want to see the anguish in her eyes. That would make it too real.

"Let's not tell each other our calls," she murmurs. "Not unless we absolutely have to or there's something we can't handle on our own."

Those words snap my eyes wide open and I turn to face her. Her eyes gleam at me from out of the darkness. She understands. We both do.

She lies so close to me....close enough for me to slip my fingers into her hair and pull her in to kiss her. "I love you," I tell her.

She kisses me back and wraps her arms around my neck. I don't want to lie here on the couch with her anymore.

I stand up, pull her legs around my waist, and she clings to me for dear life while I carry her to my bedroom—our bedroom. She'll never leave this house.

I lower her onto the mattress and she stretches out all naked and soft from sex. She arches her back where I can see her.

Excruciating love overwhelms me. I sit down on the bed next to her and stroke my hands all over her body. I don't need to do anything except sit here and admire this prize of mine.

She flares her nostrils and moans when I touch her. Her breasts stand up and her nipples harden when I squeeze them between my fingers.

I caress down her stomach, push her thighs apart, and pass my palms across her sensitive, quivering petals. Her flesh glistens with moisture just waiting for me.

I rub her and make her moan higher and louder. I love how much she wants me. The feeling that she needs me makes me feel unstoppable. I can do anything as long as she needs me like this.

I follow every graceful curve and bask in the light of aching desire in her eyes. I can make her moan for me and leave her wanting more. I always want to see that look in her eyes when she looks at me.

She flexes her hips trying to push herself into my hands, but this feels too good.

I stand up, pull down the covers, climb into bed, and draw her in next to me. I guide her down at my side where she was before.

She nestles into my arm and neck still whimpering with aching desire. She sighs and moans when her sweet box touches my leg, but she doesn't climb onto it to rub herself to another climax.

She finally shudders and sinks into the mattress. She's mine now. I can take her whenever I want to.

Chapter 19: Chris

I bend over and look at myself in the mirror. "Do I look all right?"

"You look beautiful," my brother Zack calls from the other side of the room. He barely looks up from his phone where he's been leaning his shoulder against the wall for the last hour.

My sister Lisa shoots him a death glare and turns back to me. "Don't listen to him, Chris. He's a guy. He doesn't know anything."

"So you're saying she doesn't look beautiful?" he counters. "I think I know when my little sister looks beautiful."

Lisa hovers around me straightening my veil. "You look beautiful, Chris."

"Isn't that what I just said?" Zack demands.

Ellen limps over to me. "Don't forget your earrings."

"Oh, yeah." I take them from her and put them on.

Leila, Emily, and Brooke move around the room arranging everything. They've decorated the whole firehouse for my wedding and they've set up the training room to be my dressing room. Soft music plays over the loudspeaker throughout the firehouse.

I stand in front of the mirror trying to find something wrong with my appearance, but I can't find anything.

My white sequined gown sweeps to the floor and glistens in the overhead lights. A million gems shimmer in my veil. The dress leaves my shoulders and arms bare in a simple fall of glistening brilliance. This is exactly how I wanted to look on my wedding day.

Someone knocks on the door and I hear Danny call out, "Five minutes!"

Zack sticks his phone in his pocket, comes toward me, and takes both my hands. He beams down at me. "I'm proud of you. I know you're gonna be happy."

Lisa waves her hand in front of her face. "I think I'm gonna cry!"

"At least wait until the ceremony starts," he tells her and turns back to me. "I couldn't ask for you to marry a better man. I didn't think I would ever be comfortable giving you away to anyone, but I am today." He kisses me on the cheek. "Congratulations, sweetheart. I love you."

I can only whisper, "Thanks." If this keeps up, I'm going to start crying, too.

Lisa's chiffon bridesmaid's dress rustles when she whirls away. "I can't watch this! Here. Take your bouquet, Chris."

She shoves the bouquet at me and strides away toward the training room door. Ellen, Leila, Emily, and Brooke move in and Ellen kisses me on the cheek. She's the only one of the four dressed for the wedding.

The others wear their uniforms. They're all on duty in case we get a call-out during the ceremony—or in case *they* get a call-out during the ceremony. I won't be going if they do.

"I'm so happy for you!" Ellen exclaims.

"Thanks," I murmur.

Someone knocks on the door again, but they don't say anything. Zack takes my hand. "It's time."

Ellen, Leila, Emily, and Brooke slip out of the room first. Zack's eyes shine with happiness when he slips my hand into the bend of his elbow.

Lisa positions herself at the door, sniffs a few times, wipes the tears off her cheeks, squares her shoulders, opens the door, and strides outside.

Zack escorts me to the threshold and I look out into the firehouse garage.

The crew has pulled the trucks and ambulances outside into the driveway and parked them on the street.

Rows of chairs line the garage with a red velvet carpet running between them. White flowers cover the whole opposite wall where John stands in an immaculate tux.

Josh stands in front of him with his two brothers as his groomsmen. His parents and a bunch of other relatives sit in the chairs on the right side.

His parents are both healthy, active, and super, super nice. They took me and Josh to dinner last night and his mom was so nice to me I couldn't believe she was the same woman Josh warned me about.

The rest of the firehouse crew fills the rest of the groom's side and all of the left side. Half of them are in uniform ready to leave if they need to.

The music changes from soft, melodic background music to the bridal march. The strong opening chords resound over the firehouse's speakers and everyone turns around to stare at me.

I concentrate all my attention on Josh. I don't have to think about any of these other people. This is all about him and me—no one else.

Lisa starts forward sniffing and letting out little choking sobs. She passes down the aisle to take her place on the other side of John. Now it's my turn.

Zack gives my hand a soft squeeze and we start gliding down the aisle. Josh gets closer the farther we go. His eyes command me to focus only on him.

This is the moment we've both been looking forward to—the moment we planned from when we first met. This is the moment that brings all our pasts full circle.

Zack leads me all the way up the aisle and we stop in front of Josh. He doesn't break eye contact with me when John asks, "Who gives this woman in matrimony?"

"Her sister and I do," Zack replies and Lisa bursts into tears. I hear sniffing in the seats behind me.

Zack turns to Josh. "Take care of her for me, man."

"I will," Josh replies and they hug each other.

My eyes hurt watching them, but then Zack takes my hand and places it in Josh's grasp. Now it's just the two of us.

"Dearly beloved," John begins. "We are gathered here today in the sight of God to join this man, Joshua Michael Abbott, and this woman, Christine Sophia Daniels, in the bonds of holy matrimony. If there is anyone present here today who can offer any objection to why these two should not be joined in matrimony, let him speak now or forever hold his peace."

I get so lost in Josh's eyes that I don't see anything else. We're getting married. Nothing else matters.

A different voice snaps me out of my trance. "I do! I object!"

I spin around fast and my stomach drops when I see Baxter standing in the back of the crowd. He's wearing the exact same suit he had on at the restaurant. What a prick!

He strides halfway up the aisle and stops there to glare at me and Josh. My fogged brain takes a minute to understand how anyone can hate us that much when we're both so happy.

"State your objections," John tells him. "Why do you say Josh and Chris shouldn't get married?"

"He barely knows her!" Baxter blurted out. "Chris and I lived together for five years before she moved to Howe....."

"Tell them why she moved to Howe," Zack booms out.

Baxter turns bright red and pretends not to hear. "He can't provide for her. He can't take care of her. He's at the bottom of the social ladder. He has nothing to give her. He has no ambition and no prospects."

I'm too stunned to answer. I can't believe Baxter would actually crash my wedding to insult Josh in front of all our friends and loved ones.

Before anyone can say anything, a car screeches up to the curb outside the firehouse. A blonde woman jumps out of the driver's seat, hustles up the driveway, and storms into the garage.

"Stop the wedding!" she yells. "Stop the wedding! I object!"

I cringe when I see that it's Josh's ex-fiancé, Lena. We haven't seen her since she got into the car accident on the highway and Josh told her he wasn't interested in getting back together with her.

She wears a plain blue pencil skirt, a sleeveless top, and flat white sneakers. She didn't even have the consideration to dress up to come and ruin our wedding.

"What the hell are you doing here, Lena?" Josh's mom snaps. "You don't deserve to be in the same room with Josh and Chris after the crap you pulled."

"Josh and I were made for each other!" Lena blurts out and waves at me. "He just met this woman! He barely knows her. Josh and I grew up together. We've been a couple for decades."

"Until you walked out on him," one of Josh's brothers chimes in. "It doesn't sound to me like you thought you were made for each other then."

"That was a special situation!" Lena counters. "There were extenuating circumstances."

"You're damn right there were," Josh's dad calls out. "He'd just lost his best friend in the line of duty and you had to go and pour salt into the wound by wrecking his life. Now he's happier than ever. If he goes back to you, *I'll* object."

A smile starts to creep over Josh's lips as one person after another calls out from the crowd. "Chris was the one who got you out of that car when you crashed," Sophie calls out. "You should be grateful instead of trying to wreck what's supposed to be the happiest day of her life,"

"Josh took care of you in the ambulance and then came to see you in the hospital after your car accident," Ellen adds. "I saw you afterward and you were crying about how you came to Howe to get him back, but he told you he wasn't interested. He told you he'd moved on and you ruined your relationship by abandoning him when he needed you most. You just don't want to accept the consequences of your own actions."

Baxter waves all that away and strides a few steps forward. "None of that matters. Come on, Chris. Come with me. You can't marry this idiot. He isn't worthy of you."

Gasps and yells break out from the crowd. Zack dodges into Baxter's path and straight-arms him away from me. "Don't take another step, pal. You aren't going anywhere near her."

"Go on, Baxter," Lisa calls out. "Tell everyone here why Chris moved to Howe after she spent all those happy years living with you in Portsmouth."

Baxter tries again to wave that away. "That doesn't matter. It's all in the past."

"No? I'll tell them, then," Lisa goes on. "She moved to Howe because you left her for another woman. You and Chris were engaged to be married, but you broke it off with her and shacked up with someone else within a week. She's known Josh a lot longer than you knew....whatever the hell her name was."

Baxter glares at her, but before he can answer, Danny calls out from the seats. "Josh saved Chris's life more than once. He got himself put in the hospital saving her from a violent attack in the pool hall parking lot and then he saved her again when a burning building collapsed with both of them inside it."

"I've never seen Chris as happy as she is with Josh," Naomi adds.

"Chris didn't think she would ever get together with anyone again after the mess you made of her life, Baxter," Lisa finishes. "Now she's happy again thanks to Josh."

"It looks like Josh can take better care of Chris than you can, pal," Keith calls out.

Baxter opens his mouth, but John raises his hand. "I think we've all heard enough. These objections are overruled. You two can either sit down for the rest of the ceremony or you can leave. Which will it be?"

Cheers break out behind us. I hear a few people yelling, "Go back where you came from!" and "And stay gone!" and "Eat it, you ungrateful morons!"

Baxter refuses to turn around. He glares at John and then at me and Josh. "This isn't over."

"You said that before," Josh replies. "You saying that is the reason we're here, so you saying it now probably means Chris and I will be happier and more in love than ever."

Laughter breaks out in the seats behind us. Baxter glares at us and then storms out.

Lena stands there staring at us for a second. I don't know what to say to her.

I actually feel bad for her. She had the best man in the world. She was about to marry him and start living the wonderful life that I'm going to be living from now on.

She lost that and she doesn't know what to do.

Before anyone can say anything, John starts up again. "Josh and Chris, you have come before us today to join in the bonds of matrimony in the site of your families and your community. This is a sacred oath and bond that seals your commitment to continue the legacy of unity and values our community holds dear. Let everyone here bear witness that both of you have undertaken this commitment in the spirit of building a better future for all of us."

Josh and I turn back to face him. Those words sink home. We're doing this. His words bring me back to the reason we're really here.

"Josh, do you take this woman, Chris, to be your lawfully wedded wife?" John asks. "To love, honor, and cherish her, in sickness and in health, for better or worse, for richer or poorer, for as long as you both shall live?"

Josh bursts into a massive grin. "Absolutely."

"Chris?" John asks. "Do you take Josh to be your lawfully wedded husband, to love, honor, and cherish him, in sickness and in health, for better or worse, for richer or poorer, for as long as you both shall live?"

I can't stop beaming at Josh. "I do."

John asks. "Do you have the ring?"

Josh's older brother hands him a simple gold wedding band. Josh rubs my fingers as he holds my hand.

"Repeat after me," John tells him. "'With this ring, I thee wed'."

"With this ring, I thee wed," Josh repeats and slips the ring onto my finger.

It sends a shiver up my arm and down my spine. That sensation changes everything about me. I'm not the person I was before. I'm married. I'm Josh's wife.

Excitement overwhelms me and my knees almost buckle, but I have to hold it together a little longer.

John turns to me. "Do you have Josh's ring?"

Lisa hands me Josh's ring. It's the same ring I bought for him after Lena's car accident.

Josh's whole face glows when he puts his hands in mine.

"Repeat after me," John tells me. "'With this ring, I thee wed'."

I slip the ring onto his finger. "With this ring, I thee wed."

"Then, by the power invested in me by the County of Howe, I now pronounce you man and wife," John declares. "You may kiss the bride."

Josh's eyes lock on me. This kiss will seal the deal and it will be done. Nothing will ever tear us apart after this.

At that moment, someone else bursts into tears right behind me. I barely have time to glance in that direction to see Lena whirl away and charge out of the firehouse. Did she really stand there through our whole wedding ceremony?

She disappears around the corner and vanishes out of view. I'm so stunned that I stare after her and then glance at Josh to figure out what we should do about this.

That's when I see him still staring at me. He hasn't kissed me yet.

The look on his face makes me burst into nervous giggles. We're married now. One kiss can't change that.

He steps up to me in one quick stride, slides his fingers into my hair, and kisses me hard in front of everyone.

I grab him and kiss him back just as hard. I want with everything I am to be married to him. I don't want anything else.

Another tide of cheers breaks out in the seats. People whoop and whistle and throw handfuls of rice over us.

We break apart both laughing and then wince when more rice hits us in the face. Fortunately, everyone runs out of rice pretty quickly. We can finally turn around to face our loved ones.

Josh takes my hand, grips it tight, and we race down the aisle toward the firehouse driveway. Cheers and yells follow us outside where Josh's truck sits waiting for us.

Someone has painted, *Just Married,* on both sides, covered the truck in a giant white ribbon bow tied up like a huge present, and tied a bunch of tin cans to the back bumper.

We both burst out laughing when we see it. He runs around the truck, opens the passenger door for me, and scoops up the train of my dress to help me get in.

The crowd of guests and fire crew gather at the garage entrance to wave, clap, and whistle as he gets into the cab and pulls away.

I wave from the passenger window. I won't see them for a week, and when I come back, I'll have a different name on the firehouse roster. I won't be Chris Daniels anymore. I'll be Chris Abbott—Mrs. Josh Abbott.

Josh grins at me as we drive away. He's thinking the same thing.

Just as we pass the park, I spot Baxter sitting on a bench under the trees. He's sitting next to Lena and talking to her while she sniffs into a tissue. Just as we drive past, he puts his arm around her shoulders.

Josh chuckles, extends his hand across the seat, and threads his fingers into mine. We both grin at each other. We're free.

We drive back to his house—our house—and he helps me out. "You go inside and start getting ready to go to the airport." He takes a closer look at his truck and makes a face. "I have to get this stuff off before we go anywhere else."

I giggle, lift my skirts, and go inside. We've already packed most of our stuff for our honeymoon. I just need to shower, wash the gel and glitter out of my hair, and change into some normal clothes.

I go to the bedroom and take one last look at myself in the mirror. I sure do look good in this dress.

It was a perfect wedding in every possible way, especially the part about Baxter and Lena showing up and all my and Josh's family and friends saying so many nice things about us. I'll never forget that.

Everyone we know is pulling for us. It sure is nice to know that.

I'm just taking off my veil when Josh comes in. He pulls off his tie and I turn my back to him. "Could you please unzip me, sweetheart?"

He turns to face me, but instead of unzipping me, he places his warm hands on my bare shoulders, bends in, and buries his face in my neck.

He ravages my neck down to my shoulder and crawls his hot mouth up to my ear. "I have to take you just one time in this dress. I can't let you take it off before I have you—just once."

He spins me around and attacks my mouth in maddening kisses. He kisses me fast and hard and hot, propels me backward against the wall, and in a split second, he lifts my legs off the floor and dives between them to hold me up.

I can't kiss him fast enough. He comes at me so strong and greedy that he electrifies my every nerve. He swishes my skirts up, and in seconds, he touches my panties underneath.

I gasp as his fingers find me and pull my panties aside. He's taking me in my wedding dress. I'm his wife now and he's my husband.

He crushes me against the wall and lets out low growls of cruel desire as he drives between my legs. I can already feel how hard he is.

He dives into my neck again and I gasp when those searing kisses pepper my skin down to my bare chest.

He uses both arms to hold me up and his scorching rod touches my enflamed tissues. In seconds, he plunges inside and nails me to the wall.

God damn, that feels so good! I need him so bad.

His tortured gasps and growls light me on fire and he skyrockets me into the fastest, hardest, most brutal climax of my life. I scream as his heat gushes into me and overflows me.

It's all over in a few minutes and he leans against me crushing his forehead against mine and rasping for breath. "Baby!" he croaks. "I wanted to do that ever since I saw you in that dress."

I kiss him deep and long. "I love you!"

He leans back and lowers my legs to the floor, but he doesn't let me go. He keeps me there for a long time just kissing me and rocking his body on top of me. He feels fantastic and strong and so deeply male.

He finally gives a shuddering sigh, straightens up, and his eyes clear. "Sorry. I just had to get that out."

I blush and burst into nervous laughter. "Anytime you need help with anything, I want to be the first person you call."

He laughs, too. "That's my girl—always looking out for my well-being."

We share another long, deep kiss and then he turns me away from him to unzip my dress, but when it slips off my body, he bends in close to my ear. "Maybe you should change in the other room or we'll never get to the airport."

I smirk at him. "You'll just have to control yourself for a few hours. Isn't that why you said you don't drink—so you can be as in control of yourself as possible as much of the time as possible."

He laughs and plops down on the bed. "You're right. I want to watch."

My cheeks turn bright red. "You better change, too, or we really will be late."

He grins, stands up, and starts taking off his tux. By the time he changes into his regular clothes, I'm ready to leave.

We go back outside. He's removed the bow, the paint, and the cans from his truck so we can travel incognito.

He opens the passenger door for me and I get into the seat, but neither of us can stop grinning at each other. We're married now and we're going on our honeymoon. We're about to have the most magical week of our lives before the excitement really starts.

<u>End of Book 4.</u>

If you enjoyed this book, please consider leaving a review. You can also support me on Patreon at <u>www.patreon.com/InvisiblePublishing</u>.

Keep Reading

F
irehouse Blues Series: Book 5: Haunted Past

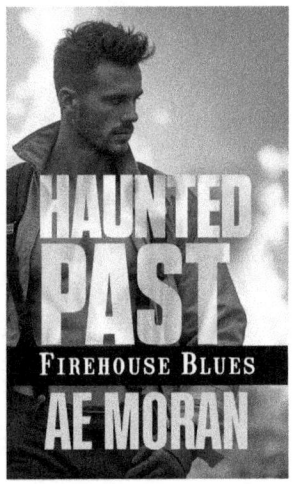

Firefighter Billy Cates might be a little rough around the edges, but no one in the Howe County Fire Department questions his dedication to saving lives and helping anyone in need. His friends and partners trust him with their lives, but everything starts to fall apart when a series of incidents threaten to derail Billy's career and the rest of his life with it.

No one knows better than paramedic Brooke Elsworth that Billy has a big heart and a big personality. They've always been friends, and when Billy's life starts to unravel, she just has to find a way to help him. She might not be able to help him when their relationship turns to something more—something neither of them is prepared to handle.

They won't be able to stop the events about to sweep their lives away and remake both of them into something they never thought possible. Can Brooke and Billy pull this runaway train back from the brink of disaster before it leaves both their lives in ruins?

You can find it at your favorite book retailer.

Get All of AE Moran's Free Books

S ign Up Once—Get all A.E. Moran's free books including brand
new releases

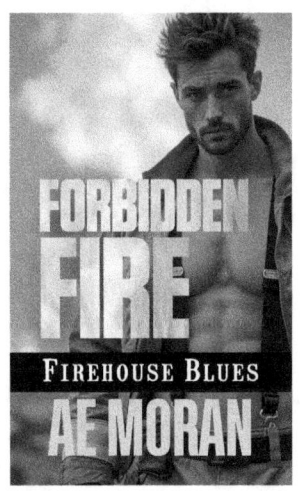

When what you want most is the one thing you can never have......

Austin McAuliffe is every woman's dream firefighter—young, strong, drop-dead hot, and selflessly dedicated to his career—and to the woman of his heart, Emma Brady. Only one other person holds a place in Austin's life—his best friend and fellow firefighter, Theo Gough. Austin insists on Theo spending time with Austin and Emma as a couple, especially when these two firefighters have a hard day at the office.

No one can believe when Austin completely flips out and randomly accuses Theo and Emma of flirting with each other in front of the whole fire crew. Could there be some deeper, more sinister reason for Austin to suddenly lose his mind and lash out at those closest to him?

Emma is devastated when Austin coldly dumps her with no warning and disappears out of her life, but Austin casts a long shadow. The nightmare of his sudden betrayal will come back to haunt Emma and Theo long after Austin is gone. Will the ghosts of the past ruin any chance for them to regain their happiness.....or will Austin's madness take down everyone he cares about along with him?

Sign up at www.authoraemoran.com to read it for free.

About AE Moran

A.E Moran is the contemporary romance pen name for Theo Mann.

I write 70 books per year—and yes, before you ask, all these books are my original creative work. Nothing written under my name is AI-generated or ghostwritten because I write better than AI and any ghostwriter out there.

People don't read fiction for entertainment or to escape from reality. People read fiction to see their humanity reflected in another person's character and story.

This is my promise to you. When you read my books, you'll see your own humanity reflected in the characters and stories. I take this commitment to my readers very seriously. My books are an intimate form of communication between us. I would never disrespect my readers by turning that over to a machine or another writer. This is my bond between me and you as my reader.

I write 20,000 words per day as my daily work output. If anyone with a public platform would like to challenge me to prove this in a controlled environment, feel free to contact me on this website's contact page.

I worked as a professional ghostwriter for fifteen years. Now I'm going for the Guinness World Record by writing 700 books over the next ten years and 1400 books over the next twenty years, all originally written by me. See my website for the full book list.

I'm also the author of *Proof for the Existence of God* and the *Crimes Against Fiction* blog. You can find all my nonfiction work at www.crimes-against-fiction.com.

If you have a story idea, or if you would like me to explore a series in more depth, or if you'd like me to explore a character by writing a spinoff series about that character or world, leave me a message on my website's contact page. I answer all reader emails, so ask me anything, tell me what you liked and didn't like, and let me know where you'd like your favorite series to go. I would love to hear your ideas and find out what you'd like to read next.

You can find out more at www.theomann.com or at www.authoraemoran.com.

Also by AE Moran (so far)

Standalone Novels

Heart on a Knife Edge

Dream Dimension

Just Friends

Back From the Dead

Damaged

Small Town Reunion

Series

Firehouse Blues (Books 1-10)

Turning Point Ranch (Books 1-10)

The Billionaires' Club (Books 1-10)